The First Robin of SPRING

NATALIE LONDON

Bella
BOOKS
2013

Bella Books, Inc.
P.O. Box 10543
Tallahassee, FL 32302

Printed in the United States of America on acid-free paper
First published 2013

Cover Designer: Linda Callaghan

ISBN 13: 978-1-59493-320-2

For Katherine B.

About the Author

Natalie London served three years with the Peace Corps in Thailand and many years as the manager of a hospital chemistry laboratory. She is a Master Gardener, Certified Beekeeper and plays the French horn, recorder and flute. Natalie and her partner live in southeast Wisconsin.

CHAPTER ONE

August 1998

I opened my eyes and sat up to look at the bedside clock. Three in the morning. I fell back, my neck damp with perspiration. Despite the open windows and the fan blowing its anemic breeze toward me, August nights in Wisconsin were hot, especially in an upstairs bedroom in an old house. It had never bothered my aunt all the years she lived here but then her bedroom had been on the first floor. I had only been living here a month and still didn't feel comfortable sleeping in her bedroom but instead slept in this upstairs bedroom which had been mine when I came to visit. Now that I owned the house maybe I could see about installing air-conditioning next spring.

The dim light of a streetlamp cast grotesque shadows on the walls and outlined the familiar heavy old furniture. I knew it wasn't the heat but the recurring dream that left me exhausted and perspiring. The fire in the lab, the flames, sirens, screams from inside as those of us who made it out watched in horror, unable to help our trapped co-workers. I closed my eyes and wished that sleep would come for a few more hours.

***

I stood in a clearing at the Green River Nature Center with my fellow birdwatchers, all of whom appeared to be at least thirty years older than my thirty-one years. My binoculars dangled from my neck as I clutched my bird identification guide in my left hand. The cool morning was beginning to warm up as the sun rose higher over the trees.

Our leader, Bill, unbuttoned his plaid wool jacket and looked us over. "Now, let's share our favorite bird with one another."

His gaze fell on me. "How about you, Julie—is that your name?"

All eyes turned toward me. "Yes, Julie. I like robins." There was a stir among the group and some looked away in embarrassment. "They are the only ones that really take a bath in my birdbath, the others just drink. I love to see them bouncing along the grass with a worm hanging from their mouths and best of all, when I see one in the spring I know the winter is over."

Bill cleared his throat. "You may not know that the American Robin is of the thrush family. They were named after the European Robin because of the male's bright red breast, though the species are not closely related." He turned to a couple standing at the front of the group. "Jim and Carol, what's your favorite?"

Some exotic, to me anyway, bird was named and there were murmurs of agreement in the group. I mentally crossed bird-watching off my list of new pursuits.

After our class Jim and Carol approached me. They wore matching tan Windbreakers and Carol had her gray hair cut in that short sensible style favored by some older women.

"Julie, are you related to Margaret Burke?"

"Yes, she was my aunt."

Carol removed her binoculars from around her neck and handed them to Jim. "I remember her talking about her niece Julia. Margaret did so much for our Nature Center, you know she was one of our founders and then with the legacy she left us, well, we've been trying to raise the funds for a new building and now we can go ahead."

Carol leaned forward and added in a confidential tone, "There's talk of naming it after her. Such a generous amount."

My aunt, at the age of eighty-three, had died suddenly of a heart attack at a church function. I had expected her to leave everything to her church and numerous other interests, like the Nature Center. Four months after her death when her will was probated I was astounded to find she had left her home and what her attorney described as a substantial amount of money to me. The church and others had all received something but I was sure it was common knowledge among my aunt's friends that I had inherited most of the money.

Carol removed her Windbreaker and handed it to Jim. "Some of us stop for breakfast after this class. Would you like to join us?"

I peered at my watch. "Thanks so much but I can't this morning."

"Maybe next time. So nice to meet Margaret's niece."

In the parking lot I climbed into my Wrangler and decided I had better go home. It wouldn't do to stop somewhere for coffee and have Jim and Carol come in and see me.

When I entered the house the phone was ringing. I dropped my book and binoculars on a chair in the kitchen and reached for the yellow wall phone.

"I got you, great, I didn't know if you'd be around."

I finally identified the voice. "Beth. Is that you? Where are you calling from?"

"I'm here in Green River but have to go back to Milwaukee this afternoon. I thought maybe we could meet for lunch."

"Sure Beth, do you have a place in mind?"

She named a health food restaurant on the west side of town.

"Is one o'clock okay?"

"Yes, see you then." I hung up puzzled as to why Beth called. She had worked in the office of the lab where I was a microbiologist but we had never been close. Outside of work, with a husband and two children, she was busy with her family.

I had a shower, got dressed and headed across town for the restaurant.

Beth was already seated at a table and waved to me as I came in. She looked crisply stylish in white linen slacks and a yellow short-sleeved print blouse. A large white leather purse emblazoned with yellow sunflowers took up the chair next to her. As usual, her makeup was perfectly applied.

As I sat down Beth looked me over. "You're looking well. Not working must agree with you."

After the fire I had quit the lab. I didn't have any plans; I just didn't want to go back there. It seemed logical to my co-workers for me to move up here to Green River since I had inherited my aunt's house. They didn't know about the money.

Beth sighed. "We are all waiting for them to rebuild the lab or move to another location. My vacation time is running out and I need the income."

Beth pushed back her long blond hair, about the same color as mine. In the lab she had been what I thought of as an organizer. Always busy taking up a collection for something or someone and planning the Christmas party and annual picnic. Her family took up much of her time and despite the lab's no solicitation policy we were always buying Girl Scout cookies or pledging money for some charity walk they participated in.

I looked around the restaurant at the plain wooden tables and chairs and the black-and-white nature photos on the walls then picked up the one page lunch menu. "Here comes the waitress."

Beth smiled. "Julie, this is 1998, they call them servers now."

We sat in silence as Beth unwrapped her napkin and silverware and then played with her fork. "Julie, I'm going to ask you for a favor."

I waited, wondering what I could do for her.

"You know Amy was living here in Green River when she disappeared."

Beth's younger sister Amy had vanished one night almost two years ago and had never been found.

"You played in that community orchestra in Milwaukee together before she moved up here to Green River so you knew her."

"Not very well, Beth. When any of us went out for drinks after a rehearsal she seldom joined us."

"But, you played in the horn section together and you sat next to her."

Beth opened her napkin and spread it on her lap as our food arrived. Iced tea and a salad for me and some kind of a rice dish for her. "After I cleaned out Amy's apartment I stored some boxes of her things in our basement. Last week I finally went through them."

I squeezed the lemon into my iced tea and waited for Beth to continue.

"There were some letters. They were what you would call love letters. I don't know who they were from, just signed with an initial. I have a feeling they were from… this is awkward." She put down her fork.

"You mean from a woman?"

Beth nodded. "Yes, from a woman."

I took a sip of my iced tea and put the glass down. "Beth, didn't you know Amy was a lesbian?"

Beth flinched, picked up her napkin and dabbed her mouth. "I suspected but never asked her. You know, it didn't come up."

I put down my fork. "So that's why you think I would have a better idea of what happened to her?"

"Oh, Julie, don't be offended. I know other gay people."

I picked up my fork again. "Now tell me what you know about Amy's disappearance."

Beth smiled in relief. "Thanks Julie." She looked across the room, frowning in an effort to remember. "Her car, an older Chevy, was still in the apartment parking lot but her purse was gone. Someone saw her in the afternoon so she must have left at night. The police thought she might have gone off with someone but she never touched her bank account and none of her clothes seemed to be missing. We don't know if she was involved with anyone because I don't know how old those letters were. After two years I'm afraid there isn't much hope anymore."

I agreed but didn't say so.

"I thought when you join the orchestra here where she played you might meet some people who knew her and would know more about her."

"Rehearsals don't start until September. I'll see what I

can find out but I'm not so sure I'll be very good at this sort of thing."

"Anything will help." Beth leaned forward. "Say, guess what? There's talk that the lab had several violations in their last safety inspection and never took care of them. They might have a big liability case on their hands."

I picked a chunk of tomato out of my salad. "I'm not surprised. I remember when I reported the frayed cord on the mixer and nothing got done."

We finished our meal and Beth insisted on paying. "It's the least I can do." She looked out the window. "Is that your Jeep Wrangler? When did you get that?"

"When I moved up here, I thought something that could handle the snow would be a good idea."

"Don't they plow the roads here in the winter?"

"I'm sure they do. I probably overreacted." I'd always wanted a Jeep. I liked the old-fashioned square lines and sporty look and although everyone had warned me against buying it I was enjoying it.

We parted in the parking lot with promises to keep in touch. As I drove home I remembered one of the only times Amy had talked about her family. There was some kind of animosity between her and them. Her mother always expected too much of her and her sister didn't understand her. I hadn't paid much attention at the time. So many people complained about their families. I didn't have a family.

CHAPTER TWO

The next morning I tied my hair back with a piece of ribbon, put on a baseball cap and carried my mug of coffee outside. The temperature was predicted to reach into the nineties so I didn't want to be working in the yard then. This was always a quiet neighborhood and now I could hear only an occasional bird chirping or insect noise. The weather was clear, already warm, and sunny. I opened the garage and took a pair of clippers off their hook on the wall, put on my gardening gloves and dragged out the yard waste bag.

My aunt's house was built in 1902 and when she

bought it in 1951 she made an effort to keep the heirloom plantings. Along the back fence were a large arching bridal wreath and two towering lilac bushes, all needing trimming. Not having any gardening experience I'd bought a book geared toward gardening in Wisconsin. This had become my bible and according to it the lilac and bridal wreath should be pruned just after flowering so I'd decided to wait until next year.

The first week I moved up here to my new home I'd picked up a brochure from the Green River Chamber of Commerce which extolled the historic downtown district, with its casual and fine dining and live entertainment including a theater guild and community orchestra. The city was home to the nationally known Northbrook College, a private liberal arts college. With a population of eighteen thousand in 1997, the city had been named after the Green River, which split the west side of the city from the east side.

"Good morning Julia." My neighbor Dorothy Rollins waved from across the yard and over her hedge.

Dorothy's house was also a Queen Anne, but larger and more ornate than my aunt's, boasting a bigger turret and longer porch. Dorothy was dressed in khaki slacks, a white golf shirt with a designer logo, and a large straw hat over her gray pageboy. She was carrying a wicker basket that held her gardening tools. For the heavier, less interesting work such as mowing, edging, fertilizing and tree trimming she employed a lawn service.

Unlike my aunt, Dorothy preferred the newer plant species and was always eager to introduce a new cultivar. She looked around her and commented, "The yard is looking good now. Margaret wasn't able to put a lot of effort into it the last few years, especially the older plantings." She pointed to some colorful pink plants. "Those garden phlox. I removed mine and put in the newer mildew-resistant cultivars."

I glanced over at the tall flowers I loved for their pleasant scent. Looking closely at their leaves I could see some were dappled with gray splotches. I sensed some competition had existed between Dorothy and my aunt over their yards.

"I don't know that much about gardening but I'm trying to learn. I spent a Saturday at the botanical gardens in some classes and I've been doing some reading." I did not want to sustain the rivalry.

Before I could continue, amid wild high-pitched yapping, Dorothy's Chihuahua Pepe flew out of the bushes heading for my bare legs. Dorothy dropped her basket, bent down and scooped up Pepe, saving my ankles. The dog continued his fierce barking, threatening to leap out of Dorothy's arms.

"Now, be a good boy. You know your neighbor Julia."

From past experience I knew better than to reach out to pet him. Maybe my soothing voice could calm him.

"Hi Pepe, are you a good boy?"

More barking which Dorothy ignored. "You know Julia, if you have the time the college has a horticulture program. Take some classes this fall."

"That might be interesting. I'll check on it."

Dorothy looked up at the large oak tree in the yard. "Be careful, I see some dead branches up there. Think about those classes." She picked up her basket and left for the other side of her house carrying the protesting Pepe under her other arm.

I pulled a few weeds and walked around the house. Tall lacy ferns covered the foundation on the north side and now that it was August, snowball hydrangeas on the south held lime green flowers. I had just mowed the lawn a few days ago so I put away my tools and went into the house.

As I poured cereal into a bowl I thought about Dorothy's suggestion. After I quit the lab I had looked forward to not working, but after a month I was feeling lost without the daily routine and sense of identity the job had provided. I had planned to go over to the college to sign up for the community orchestra they sponsored. Maybe I would look at the class schedule while I was there.

As the afternoon temperature and humidity rose I descended to the cool basement. This seemed like a good time to start cleaning it out. It consisted of one large room interrupted periodically by sturdy pillars. A gas furnace had replaced the coal furnace years ago but the stained outline of the old furnace remained on the floor. My aunt had replaced the ancient wringer wash machine and added a dryer but the washtubs still stood. I decided to start two piles, items for the charity thrift store and those for the trash. Weeks ago I had sorted through most of my aunt's personal effects, giving the coats, suits and shoes to Goodwill.

Looking around I decided to start with the junk. I soon had a pile consisting of an old fan with a frayed cord, a bundle of dirty clothesline rope and paint cans with their spilled contents dried on the labels. I added remnants of rolls of wallpaper, a wooden chair missing a rung and a beat-up card table. Against the wall stood two suitcases. I unzipped the plaid soft-sided case to make sure it was empty and put it in the donation pile. The other was a heavy leather case with mildew damage. I unlatched it and pushed back the cover. Inside were bundles tied with red ribbon. I picked up a bundle and pulled out a letter. The postmark was Iron Mountain, Michigan and the year was 1965. I inspected other bundles. The last postmark seemed to be 1970.

I opened the envelope and scanned the letter. The writer talked of the happiness they both felt when they were last together, the touch of her hand...I stopped reading. This was a love letter and signed only by the initial L, written with an elaborate loop at the top and bottom. The paper was cream-colored with a deckle edge and the handwriting was unmistakably a woman's. I put the letter back feeling I had intruded on something personal, then stood up and looked around for a trash bag to discard the letters but couldn't find one. Stiff from kneeling on the damp floor, I decided to bring a trash bag the next time I came down here.

As I climbed the stairs I remembered the letters to Amy that Beth had found. They too had only been signed by an initial. Was that how people signed love letters? I didn't know, never having received any.

***

The next morning I drove over to Northbrook College to register for the orchestra and look at the horticulture class schedule.

The school sat on acres of manicured green lawns and wooded areas, the buildings reflecting the various periods of the school's history. The original stately three-story stone buildings dated from the college's founding in 1899, the sprawling one-story brick buildings had been built since then and the modern Union and Fine Arts Building with the Stofer Concert Hall was added in the late 1980s.

A counselor for the horticulture program shook hands with me and I sat in his office. A bearded man named Jeff, he was casually dressed in a plaid shirt and jeans. He leaned back in his chair with his hands laced behind his head and told me, "You'll love the program. We have people from all different levels. Some have worked in the field for years, others with no experience. I see you have a degree in biology. Did you work in that field?"

"I worked in the microbiology department of a reference lab."

"Good, so just have your transcripts sent here."

We looked at the schedule and I decided on

Introduction to Horticulture, Exterior Plant Pests and a two-credit class entitled Fungi.

After I had taken care of the classes, stood in line for a parking permit and visited the bookstore, I went to the Continuing Education Office to sign up for the community orchestra.

A thin woman with unrealistically red hair and wire-rimmed glasses produced a registration form but held it back. "Have you called Professor Read to tell her your instrument and what part you want to play?" The college identification badge hanging around her neck read "Elsie.".

"No. Am I supposed to?"

"She likes to know before the first rehearsal who will be auditioning for the principal chairs."

"I don't want to audition, just play whatever part they need."

She frowned. "I suppose she can call you if she has a question about your part. What instrument?"

"Horn. French horn."

She handed over the form and a pen. "Good, always in demand."

I bent over the form on the counter and began filling it out. Elsie left me to greet another woman.

"Professor de Gramont," she gushed. "I hope you are registering for orchestra, we certainly need you."

I looked over to see an attractive woman with glossy medium-length dark hair, stylishly dressed in tan slacks and a black sweater. She shifted the briefcase in her hand and glanced in my direction as I lowered my gaze to the form.

"I didn't mean to wait until now to register, I've been so busy."

Elsie produced a form. "Don't worry, we still have people registering." She looked significantly in my direction.

The professor looked over at me, smiled, and then

went back to her form. She quickly filled it out. "Thanks, Elsie." She turned and left.

Elsie carried the form over and collected mine. "You'll enjoy the orchestra, Professor Read will call you."

When I got home I rode my bike around the neighborhood for almost an hour. Tomorrow I would take it out to the bike path near the Nature Center for a change of scene. I was enjoying having the time for all this outdoor exercise but was now looking forward to my classes and the interest and structure they would provide.

Now that I was committed to playing in the orchestra I got out my horn for a little practice. Just before my second year of high school my mother had decided to move from our small town with a population of five thousand down to Milwaukee. From a school where I had known my classmates since kindergarten I found myself in a high school of eight hundred students where I knew no one. I was shy and not good at making friends, but since I had always played in the school band I joined the band at my new school and then found that this school also had an orchestra. In the orchestra I not only discovered classical music but also made some friends. Music had been my salvation then and was still an important part of my life now.

I opened the book of Kopprasch etudes, warmed up and then spent forty minutes practicing them.

Now it was time for a glass of wine. I carried it to the table outside the backdoor on the small brick patio. One of my first purchases had been the round table, chairs and a Cinzano umbrella. I sipped my wine and looked with pleasure at the yard. This was beginning to feel like home.

***

Sometime during the night, I awoke with my face and neck damp with perspiration, the sheet and blanket pushed aside. It was the dream again. There were the flames, screams, sirens, but this time I was trying to get back in the building. This had not actually happened, everyone who got out had been lucky and there were no thoughts of going back in.

I turned over and tried to think of something to occupy my mind until I could fall asleep again. I pictured the good-looking professor who had registered for the orchestra and how I felt when she looked at me and smiled. There was something special in her smile, a certain warmth and intelligence. But I knew the type; probably married to a tall, handsome, self-assured man. He would be an executive or an attorney and their photo would appear in the society column of the Sunday paper attending a charity ball or fundraiser. They would have two lovely children, a boy and a girl.

Even if none of this was true I couldn't think about a relationship with anyone. I had too many of my own problems.

CHAPTER THREE

Dr. Elisabeth de Gramont, known to her friends as Lily, closed the front door to her apartment, dropped her briefcase on the floor, and sank into a leather chair to examine the mail in her hand. Two bills and an announcement of an upcoming seminar. Her phone rang. As she picked it up she saw there was a message on her answering machine.

"Lily, glad I got you. Aren't you returning to the orchestra? I saw you hadn't signed up. I left you a message this morning."

"I registered this afternoon, Vickie," she said tersely. "I've been busy with the start of the school year."

"Oh good. We need our principal flute and you know I was worried that you harbored some resentment about... what happened."

"No, Vickie, not at all," she said with deliberate carelessness.

"So, Lily, how was your summer? Did you go anywhere?" The question was polite, cautious.

"A one-week seminar in Madison. How about you, Vickie?"

"We went to the Peninsula Music Festival for a concert, spent a week. So inspiring, wonderful piano soloist."

In the awkward pause that followed, Lily wondered who the "we" referred to.

"I better let you go. See you next week." Vickie ended the conversation in her usual abrupt manner.

Lily set her mail aside and went into the kitchen. The remainder of a rotisserie chicken for a sandwich on whole wheat bread with lettuce seemed the easiest choice for dinner, and she put it together, carried it into the living room and turned on the television for the evening news, which was still full of Bill Clinton and his affair with Monica Lewinsky.

Vickie. Dr. Victoria Regina Read. Lily shuddered.

They had met at a reception for new faculty members when Lily had begun at the college three years ago. Vickie, who had been at the school for six years as chairman of the music department, held a very high opinion of herself, which others apparently shared. Everyone catered to her, tiptoed around her.

That evening Vickie made a dramatic entrance into the hall wearing a cape, which she removed with a flourish and tossed onto a chair. She and Vickie had connected at the wine table. Lily had just picked up a glass of something red and dry. She preferred white wine but had recently read that red was supposed to be better for your health, so was trying to switch. She had just taken a sip when up came Vickie to the bar.

"What wines do you have? What are the labels?" she demanded of the bartender.

The young bartender awkwardly examined the bottles and read off their labels. Vickie tapped her foot impatiently. "I'll have the merlot." The one red wine Lily did not care for.

Vickie coolly looked her over, and then approached her. Vickie was not conventionally attractive but very handsome with her long thick chestnut hair pulled back and her intense brown eyes. Tall and willowy, she turned her commanding appearance on Lily.

"How do you like the school? Where were you before this?"

As she answered the peppering of questions, Lily found herself captivated.

Eventually this led to meeting for a drink, dinner, a concert, and then an invitation to Vickie's home where they made love for the first time. At first it was exciting and Lily was desperately in love, then the demands started to become wearing and exhausting. Vickie was imperious about what she wanted in and out of bed and then there were the phone calls in the middle of the night when she'd had one too many nightcaps.

Then Lily discovered Vickie was also sleeping with a woman from the orchestra.

That had been two years ago. Now her life had settled into a comfortable routine. After getting over the hurt and humiliation she had determined to be far more cautious if there ever was a next time.

Later she took a shower and as she dried herself she looked at her body in the mirror and blushed remembering how Vickie had admired her breasts. The attention she had lavished on them.

After the breakup, with more time on her hands, she had devoted herself to her work in the English department and to keeping fit, working out at the college exercise facility, swimming and walking. This year, at thirty-six, she had replaced running with walking after watching her colleagues, only a few years older than she, hobbling around talking of knee and hip replacements.

Lily tied the belt of her terry cloth robe, went into the kitchen and poured a glass of white wine. In the living room she put on a CD of the Nielsen *Flute Concerto*.

Settled in her leather chair she lifted the wineglass thinking about the woman she had seen in the Continuing Education Office signing up for the orchestra. She had the combination of blond hair and blue eyes that Lily had always admired, but there was also something appealingly vulnerable in her expression when she looked at Lily.

Abruptly she set down her wineglass and pushed the thought of the woman from her mind. Not again.

CHAPTER FOUR

I sped in my Wrangler down the highway on a mild, sunny day. It was the last Saturday of August and I was headed to Milwaukee to close up my apartment and turn in the key. The lease expired at the end of August and I had already moved or discarded everything including my furniture, which was mostly hand-me-downs or what I thought of as starter furniture. My aunt had some nice pieces in the house and I intended to keep them and replace those I didn't care for.

I was at the apartment and doing a little final cleaning when the phone rang.

"Saw your Jeep. When did you get here?"

"Hi Ginger. A couple of hours ago. I'm here until Monday morning, the lease is up in a few days."

"Good thing I caught you. Some of us from the lab are getting together tonight at our place for pizza and beer. You can come can't you?"

Ginger and Cindy lived in my building and still worked at the lab. I wasn't eager to relive our experience in the fire but being in the same apartment complex made it difficult to refuse, especially if they saw I'd stayed home.

"Sure, what time?"

At six thirty I rang their bell carrying two bottles of wine. Besides Ginger and Cindy there were two other women who looked vaguely familiar.

Cindy motioned in their direction. "You know Bev and Marie."

I waved, remembering them from the front office. The air was already thick with smoke, and a CD of some woman's band was blaring from the speakers at the end of the living room. I already regretted coming but once I had a glass of wine in my hand and found a chair with the least amount of dog hair on it I began to relax.

Ginger carried her bottle of beer into the living room and sat on the floor, extending her long legs. With her bright red hair and freckles, Ginger was an appropriate nickname. I couldn't recall her real name, something like Genevieve.

"What are you doing for excitement up in Green River?" Ginger tipped the beer bottle back and took a long drink.

What could I tell them? Riding alone on bike trails or my experience with the bird-watchers? That would be guaranteed to provoke teasing and laughter.

"I signed up for some horticulture classes at the college."

"Really?" Cindy frowned. "Since when are you interested in plants?" Her dark hair and suntan were a contrast to Ginger as was her quieter demeanor.

"I've been working in the yard and garden and just realized I have an affinity for them."

"Are you looking for a job up there?" Bev pushed back her grown-out perm, lit a cigarette and blew the smoke my way.

"Not right now." They knew I had inherited the house, but not the money.

"Lucky you. You know the lab is finally going to reopen in three weeks."

Ginger set her bottle down and lit up a cigarette. "But somewhere out in Brown Deer. Everyone is upset, now they have to drive across town. I don't know why they couldn't have kept it on the south side."

Looking at Ginger and Cindy I envied them their close, comfortable relationship, something I had never been able to achieve. There had been an on-again, off-again relationship with a classmate on the basketball team at the university, which ended when we graduated and she took off for California, leaving me behind. Four years ago I met a social worker in a bar. We had a six-month affair but it ended when we discovered that except for the sex, we had nothing in common.

I tried to change the subject from talk of the lab. "I saw Beth, she was in Green River and we had lunch together."

"We invited her but she had some family thing going on. Was she up there about Amy?"

There had always been some rivalry between Ginger and Beth. It seemed to involve things like who would take up the Sunshine Club collection or run the United Way campaign.

"I'm not sure, but she wants me to try to find out anything I can about Amy's disappearance."

Marie waved her glass. "Oh, good luck. Amy was a handful. You could start with the bars, except I suppose they don't have any gay bars up there."

Cindy brought another bottle of beer for Ginger. "I think she took off with somebody. Probably is in California or Florida. She always liked warm weather."

I drank the last of my wine. "But she left everything behind including her bank account and her car."

Cindy stood up. "I'll turn on the oven for the pizza. Her bank account wouldn't amount to anything. She was a big spender and always had a different job as a bartender or waitress and I heard she left a lot of unpaid bills. Her car was a junker. I remember one door was a different color."

Server, I thought, not waitress. "I'm sure they monitored her credit card for any activity." I stood up. "Wine anyone?"

Bev held out her glass. "She could have stopped using it and applied for a different one."

I refilled our glasses and handed one to Bev. She looked at me appraisingly. "Have you met anyone interesting?"

"Not really." The good-looking professor didn't count. She had only smiled at me.

Bev accepted her glass. "Sounds like a pretty dull place there."

I took an immediate dislike to her. How dare she insult my town?

Just then a large white dog bounded into the room. Everyone grabbed for her bottle or glass.

"Gertrude. Sit." Ginger lunged for Gertrude who unfortunately did not appear to have passed her obedience class. By the time she was under control, we were all laughing and Amy and my life in Green River were forgotten.

After three large glasses of wine we finally ate the pizza

and I was ready to go back to my apartment and to bed, which tonight consisted of a pillow and blanket on the floor.

The next morning I awoke late with a pounding headache and stiff back. My makeshift bed didn't provide much support and I wasn't used to drinking so much. I got dressed and went off on my Sunday morning routine for the last time. At a nearby coffee shop I bought a large coffee, a big Danish pastry and the Sunday paper to take back to my apartment.

I went for a last run in the nearby park and in the early afternoon drove slowly around the east side inspecting smaller Queen Anne homes similar to mine. I examined their colors and landscaping. My aunt's house looked superior in comparison. She had painted it a pale cream color trimmed with white, disdaining the garish pastel colors I disliked.

Without thinking I found myself driving to the south side and pulling up in front of the lab. I must have had some idea that if I saw it again it might help bring me closure. I got out of the Jeep and stood on the sidewalk.

After two months the plywood boarding up the windows was already starting to weather and a large portion of the roof was gone. Weeds had taken over the formerly immaculate lawn. The only difference was that the acrid smoke smell had dissipated.

"There was a bad fire there."

Startled, I spun around. Standing next to me was a woman holding the leash of a small black shorthaired dog. She was wearing a nylon jacket with Jim's Tap on the back and a plastic rain scarf over her wispy brown hair.

"Yes, I know."

She peered at me through thick glasses. "You didn't work there did you?"

I nodded.

"You were lucky to survive. I live up the street. What a

terrible morning that was. All those flames." She pulled the dog back from the lawn. "I hope they tear it down, such an eyesore. Too much damage."

I put my hands in my jacket pockets. A strong breeze had come up and I felt drops of rain fall on my face.

The woman looked up at the sky. "We better go, nice to talk to you. Come on Jimmy." She tugged at the dog's leash and rapidly walked away.

That evening I ate Chinese carryout with a plastic fork and thought about my past four years in this apartment. I had been busy playing in the orchestra and in a woodwind quintet, which had disbanded when two members criticized one another's playing and a third dropped out to contest a messy divorce. There had been my physical activities: running, biking, hiking and cross-country skiing. But looking back I realized I had been lonely. My work at the lab had become increasingly dissatisfying and I had begun to have concerns about safety and procedural issues.

I set the carton of food aside and watched the rain splattering against the windows. How could there be any closure when I saw that horribly destroyed building? Seeing it had only revived all the memories.

CHAPTER FIVE

The second Monday in September I entered Stofer Hall in the Fine Arts Building fifteen minutes before the seven o'clock orchestra rehearsal. Climbing the steps to the stage, carrying my horn case and briefcase, I saw two other women with horns sitting in the last row, in front of the percussion. All day I had been nervous about the rehearsal, wondering why I put myself through this, then remembering the excitement and satisfaction of performing.

Amid the din of instruments warming up and the talk between players I approached the two horn players wondering how I would be received. They stopped their conversation.

"Good. Another horn." A plump woman with short curly blond hair looked me over. "I'm Terri." She motioned to the other woman. "This is Katy."

"Hi. I'm Julie." I set my case down, not sure which chair to take.

"Are you auditioning for first horn?" Terri dripped oil on her third valve.

"No, I'm not interested. I only want to play whatever part you need."

"Karen is our first, I usually play second or third, Katy likes fourth. Why don't you play second?"

"That's fine." I took my horn out of its case and sat down. In parts for four horns, third was usually next to first in importance. I looked up to see a pale, thin woman with short dark hair standing next to me holding a horn case.

"This is Julie." Terri motioned toward me. "She's going to play second."

Karen set her case down and opened it. "Aren't you auditioning for first?"

"Absolutely not. I'll play whatever part you need."

Karen sat down with her horn on her lap and smiled for the first time.

I looked around at the other orchestra members. I had read that the minimum age for the orchestra was eighteen but except for a couple of violin players who appeared to be in their early twenties, most of the members were middle-aged and one or two of the second violins were probably in their upper seventies. Most seemed to know one another and were amicably chatting together.

I wondered which woman was Professor Read. Standing in front of the orchestra was a stocky man with thin sandy hair and a nervous smile. I turned to Karen.

"Where's Professor Read?"

She looked around. "Not here I guess. That's Alan, her

assistant. He's nice, but as for his conducting, well you'll see."

Alan tapped on the stand with his baton. "Hi everyone. Before we start I want to introduce the new members. Please stand up so we can see you." He examined a sheet of paper he held in his hand and introduced several new string players, managing to mispronounce a few of their last names.

"Two more trombones, that's great." Two young men stood up. "Another trumpet." A man with a beard and wearing a wrinkled denim shirt stood and waved his horn. Each new member received his or her obligatory smattering of applause. Looking around I counted at least fifty musicians.

"And another French horn. Julia Burke." As I rose holding my horn the woodwind players turned in their chairs to see me. I looked up and my eyes met those of the professor from the Continuing Education Office. She smiled faintly as she briefly clapped.

Alan put the paper down, evidently relieved to have done his duty. "Let's tune, then we'll start with the 'Rosamunde Overture'."

A few minutes later I understood what Karen meant about Alan's conducting. We played about twelve measures, stopped, he corrected something, we started and then we stopped again.

By intermission I was hardly warmed up. Terri emptied the water from her horn. "This is ridiculous. I hope Professor Read gets here soon."

Almost on cue, a tall woman entered the room. She wore slacks and a short wool jacket over a turtleneck; her long hair was pulled back at her neck. Everyone's attention went to her.

"Oh good, there's Professor Read." Terri went off to talk to one of the cello players.

I stood up to stretch my legs, cradling my horn. Alan

came over to Katy and they moved away to talk together. Karen had disappeared so I sat down, not having anyone to talk to.

The intermission ended and Professor Read stepped in front of the group. I noticed there was an immediate silence; she didn't have to ask for attention.

"How wonderful to see you all and so many new members. With the added brass and percussion I have decided on a different symphony for our next concert. We will have the music next week. Dvorak's *Fourth Symphony*. For those of you who don't have a recording, bring a blank tape and Alan will record it for you."

The trombones were dismissed and then we tuned and started the Beethoven Piano Concerto No. 1. As was the custom, the soloist wouldn't be joining us until the dress rehearsal. When we had all made it through the piece I had a real respect for Professor Read's conducting and could tell I was not alone.

After the first movement Professor Read turned back several pages of her score. "Second violins. Before letter A, if you have trouble playing the four sixteenths in the group, just play the first and third notes as eighths."

Several of the older second violins nodded gratefully and picked up their pencils.

After the rehearsal I asked Terri, "Do they charge admission for the concerts?"

"Oh sure. Until last year it was three dollars, then it went up to five. Professor Read wasn't pleased, but it was the board's decision. Guess they wanted more revenue."

As Terri put her music in her case a program fell out. I picked it up to hand it back to her.

"Thanks, that's our last concert." She reached for it.

"May I see it?"

"Sure." She emptied her horn and fit it into its case.

I turned to the personnel. Under the flute section was Elisabeth de Gramont, Principal. So that was the flute-playing professor's name. "Thanks." I handed the program to Terri.

"I have to clean this stuff out. Say, we usually go out for a drink and a little something to eat after the rehearsal. I wasn't sure about tonight but it seems several are going. And Alan and Professor Read are coming, believe it or not."

Katy spoke up. "Probably wants to bond with us." She turned to me. "Want to join us?"

"Yes, I would."

Twenty minutes later, eleven of us were seated at a long table in Dos Amigos, a Mexican restaurant and bar. Across the table and at the end Professor Read was holding court.

"I know the Dvorak is an ambitious undertaking but I feel it will challenge us."

Heads nodded. Professor Read continued, "We need a harp but luckily Joanne's daughter is a harp student and has agreed to drive up here for the dress rehearsal and possibly another rehearsal."

Joanne, who I recognized from the viola section, beamed. The talk then turned to who had a child studying music.

On my left, Terri was consuming a plate of nachos. She said, "We usually have more fun but I think with Professor Read being here everyone is on their good behavior." She picked up another chip. "The rehearsal went pretty well don't you think?"

"Yes, I thought so," As I looked around at the colorful pseudo-Mexican décor my mind drifted back to the rehearsal. There were several excellent players and from what I had heard, Elisabeth de Gramont was an accomplished flutist. She played with a rich full tone and good intonation. In comparison, the second flute player sounded sharp to me in several passages and once Professor Read tactfully suggested she pull out her headjoint to lower the pitch.

I looked up to see Professor Read gazing at me. To my dismay she stood up and started toward me. Carrying her wineglass, she sat in the empty chair next to me. Was I in trouble for not calling her?

She set her glass of red wine in front of her, leaned an arm on the table and looked at me.

"So Julia, are you new in town?"

I shifted my feet uncomfortably. "I moved here about two months ago."

"So you moved here with your husband?"

"I'm not married. My aunt left her house to me."

She sipped her wine. "Whom did you play with before coming here?"

"The Municipal Symphony Orchestra in Milwaukee."

"Aren't you interested in auditioning for first?"

"No, Karen is doing a great job." I tried to think of a new subject. "Someone I played horn with in Milwaukee moved up here and played for you."

"Really, who was that?"

"Amy Leland."

Professor Read abruptly set her glass down, almost spilling the contents. "Tragic, her disappearance." She pulled the sleeve of her jacket back to examine her watch, a stylish curved oblong with a maroon leather band. "It's getting late, I have to go." She stood up, apparently having lost interest in me.

I watched her say goodbye to the rest of the group, protest when she wasn't allowed to pay her share, and go out the door. Her departure seemed to put an end to the evening. We settled the bill and left.

As I drove down the dark quiet streets of my neighborhood I tried to examine my feelings about Professor Read. She was attractive in the way some talented and intelligent people are, but I suspected she was also a complex person. More than I could cope with.

CHAPTER SIX

October had arrived bringing the first frost and then days of unending rain. My summer clothes were put away; my bicycle was hanging in the garage; and with the change in the weather I decided to move indoors and use the exercise facility at the college. On a dreary damp Friday afternoon as I was leaving the workout room I saw the flute-playing professor enter carrying her gym bag. She didn't see me and since we had never met I had no excuse to approach her.

Monday afternoon I sat in my Exterior Plant Pest class

watching a film on the Plant Disease Triangle. I found I was enjoying all my horticulture classes and looked forward to them and to spending my evenings studying and writing papers. After the film ended it was break time and most of the class raced outside for a cigarette or to get a can of soda. As I walked along in the hallway stretching my legs I thought about my promise to Beth to investigate Amy's life in Green River. So far I had gotten nowhere so perhaps at orchestra rehearsal tonight I should approach Terri and see what she knew about Amy.

That evening our rehearsal began on time with everyone present despite the pouring rain. Professor Read, looking very smart in a black turtleneck sweater and gray slacks, praised us all for turning out in the wet weather this evening and then let Alan rehearse the "Rosamunde Overture" while she sat in the back of the orchestra. It made me uncomfortable to know she was sitting so close behind me.

I wondered if she had given Alan advice about his conducting because now we went a little longer before he stopped us. When he finished she walked to the front of the orchestra, passing us and commenting, "Good job horns."

As usual, when Professor Read took over conducting the Dvorak the tone of the rehearsal changed and everyone played his or her best.

By the time we finished rehearsing the Dvorak the orchestra was exhausted but exhilarated. Now at the break several players crowded around Professor Read and I thought this might be the time to approach Terri about Amy.

"I played horn with someone who moved up here and joined this group."

Terri scanned the room for someone to talk to. "Oh, who was that?"

"Amy Leland." I watched Terri's response.

She turned around and looked at me, frowning. "Yes, she played here. Was she a friend of yours?"

"No, I hardly knew her. I only played with her."

Terri seemed to relax. "Her first week with the orchestra she auditioned for first chair. Alan did the audition and gave it to her. Then they dated for a while after that but I guess something happened or she just lost interest in him. He was kind of upset."

To keep her talking I asked, "So was there trouble about the audition?"

Terri rolled her eyes. "Was there ever. We had this woman, Marcy, who had played first for quite a few years and, boy, was she upset when Alan gave the chair to Amy. She complained to Professor Read but she told her it had been Alan's decision and she couldn't overrule him."

"What happened to Marcy?"

"She was so mad she quit the orchestra. Then when Amy disappeared two weeks before the concert we were left without a first. I couldn't take over, my father was sick and I was running to the hospital every night with no time for extra practice."

"Sounds like a mess."

"It was. Alan called Marcy and she refused to come and help out for the concert. Can't say I blamed her. In the end Professor Read had to call in a ringer and she hates to do that. She feels this is a community orchestra and we should perform with the personnel we have. I heard Marcy is playing with the Green Bay Symphony. She probably has a long commute for rehearsals, but Green Bay, they're pretty good. Lucky we have Karen now."

Terri stood up and laid her horn on her chair, sending a message that she had lost interest in the Amy Leland saga. Seeing four violin players passing around a large bag of potato chips, she headed in their direction.

When the rehearsal ended I was packing up my horn and music while next to me Karen zipped her jacket up to her chin, put the hood up and picked up her horn case. "They say it's really pouring out there. See you next week, Julie."

Now that I hadn't challenged her she was comfortable with me and we played well together.

At the door leading to the parking lot I found a group of orchestra members peering out the door and milling around. "I'm not going out in that," said one of the cello players and moved away from the door.

I made my way over. The rain was blowing in sheets; tree limbs were swaying and flashes of lightning illuminated the sky. I could see small branches littering the ground.

"Let's go to the Rathskeller and wait it out." The first clarinet, a tall woman with a frizzy perm, turned away from the door. A chorus of "great idea" and "let's go" followed this suggestion.

I turned around and standing behind me was the flute-playing professor.

"Should we go too?" This was addressed to me.

I looked out at the storm then back to her. "Yes, let's."

We followed the group already headed to the Rathskeller, a pub in the basement of the Union connected to the Fine Arts Building by an enclosed passageway.

In the Rathskeller we found ourselves sitting opposite each other at the remaining table for two with a glass of beer in front of each of us. The flute-playing professor had taken off her jacket and draped it over the back of her chair.

"I know we haven't met. I'm Lily de Gramont." She smiled and put out her hand.

I could hardly speak. "Julie Burke. Nice to meet you."

"Alan introduced you as Julia. Which do you prefer?"

"When my mother was displeased with me I was Julia. I prefer Julie."

She smiled. "Julie it is."

Across the room the clarinet player came back to her table carrying two baskets of popcorn. Lily—I now had a new name for her—twisted in her chair to look at the popcorn machine.

"Would you like some popcorn?"

"Yes. I'll get it."

She stood up. "No, I'm closer."

As I watched her walk back carrying the basket of popcorn, I admired her dark hair, cut to just above her shoulders and framing her high cheekbones and fine features and complementing her graceful, slender body. Tonight she was wearing black slacks and a plum colored sweater, which accentuated that body. She sat down and put the basket on the table.

I picked up a piece of popcorn. It looked like a snowman.

"So Julie, have you lived here in Green River long?"

I looked into her dark eyes and put the snowman in my mouth. "I moved up here from Milwaukee in July. My aunt left me her home."

She picked up a piece of popcorn. "I thought I saw you on campus."

"I enrolled in some horticulture classes. I have a biology degree and worked in the microbiology department of a lab. I needed a change. I find I'm enjoying it."

"They have a well-recognized horticulture program here." With that, Lily picked up her glass and sipped her beer.

I picked up a piece of popcorn that resembled an octopus.

She set her glass down. "Do you have family here?"

I realized we were now in the getting-to-know-you stage. The octopus went into my mouth. "No, my mother died the summer after I graduated from high school. I stayed in Milwaukee and went to the University of Wisconsin-Milwaukee. When I had breaks and holidays I stayed with my aunt. She was my father's older sister. He died when I was ten. After my first year at the university she took me to Europe that summer for three weeks. She was awfully good to me."

"She must have loved you very much to leave her home to you."

It was my turn. "Do you have any family?" How did I know that she wasn't married to that perfect imaginary man?

"My brother and his family live in Seattle. We don't see each other very often."

She took another sip of her beer. "What do you think of the orchestra?"

"I'm very impressed, there are some fine musicians and Professor Read is such a good conductor. Probably the best I've played under."

"Vickie is very talented."

Vickie? They must be good friends. Or maybe all the professors were close and on a first-name basis.

Lily turned to look across the room at the group of orchestra members who were talking and laughing loudly. I wondered if she wished she were sitting at their table. My gaze fell on her breasts. Very nice. She turned back to our table. In confusion I abruptly picked up my beer glass almost spilling it.

"I'm glad I'm not sitting over there." She shifted in her chair, crossing her legs. "Your horn section is the best since I joined the orchestra. The horn calls in the first movement of the Dvorak are beautiful."

"Thank you. We seem to get along well, not always the case with other groups I played with."

"When I came here I was so glad to find an orchestra to play with. The principal flute had just moved away and no one else wanted the chair so I kind of fell into it."

"You didn't have to challenge anyone for it." I thought of Amy.

"I wouldn't have. I'm content just playing. I guess I'm not very competitive."

"I know you're a professor here but I'm not sure of what."

"Associate professor of English. American Literature."

I was interested in knowing more but before I could ask any further questions the clarinet player came back into the room from checking the weather.

"It's let up. We better make a break for it while we can," she announced loudly as she tipped back her beer glass and drank it dry. Everyone at her table pushed back their chairs, and headed for the door.

"I guess we should go too." Lily put on her jacket and we followed the others outside to the dimly lit parking lot.

We stood together. "Good night, I've enjoyed talking to you, Julie." She moved off toward a car that looked like something small and domestic.

That night as I lay in my bed trying to fall asleep I went over every detail of my conversation with Lily, as I now thought of her. But I knew it was coincidence that we ended up at a table together at the Rathskeller and she had really only been trying to be polite by talking with me.

Then I thought about what Terri had told me about Amy. From what I was learning, Amy was not turning out to be a likable person.

CHAPTER SEVEN

I stood in the doorway and surveyed my aunt's bedroom. Originally, it had been a parlor but several years ago she had converted it into her bedroom to avoid climbing the stairs. Now I wanted to reclaim it as a den or office. Facing me was her massive bedroom set. Ornately carved from some kind of wood, it consisted of bed, dresser, chest and nightstand. This was too valuable to give away, but how to get rid of it? Perhaps an ad in the paper. I sat down and wrote out a simple advertisement for the classified section. How much to ask? I had seen advertisements for new bedroom sets for over one thousand dollars but would anyone want this? I decided on two hundred and fifty dollars, then changed it to three hundred, went to the phone and called the paper to place the ad.

Realizing I would have to clean out the drawers, I got a trash bag and pulled up a chair to the dresser. Earlier, I had disposed of all the clothing but there still remained papers, manila envelopes full of news clippings, old receipts and a lot more.

I went through the drawers discarding everything and then I picked up a picture. It was of a group of eight taken before a large body of water. I turned it over. In my aunt's handwriting was written: "Bay of Naples, July 1956." Following this were the names of the people in the picture. Standing to the left of my aunt was a pretty woman who looked vaguely familiar. I followed the listing of the names to Laura Gorman.

I set the picture aside, went down to the basement and opened the old leather suitcase. I removed the manila envelope with the pictures and carried it upstairs. The pictures were all of my aunt with another woman. Shorter than my aunt, with lighter hair, the woman was unmistakably Laura Gorman. Her letters, which had been postmarked Iron Mountain, Michigan, had suddenly ended in 1970. Had she died? If so, why was there no obituary notice in my aunt's papers? I had found many death notices for her friends in the top drawer, but none with Laura Gorman's name. Did she still live in Iron Mountain?

I went to the phone and called information for the town. No listing for Laura Gorman. I asked the operator, "Do you have any other Gorman listed?"

"Just one. Thomas Gorman."

"May I have that number? It might be the one I'm looking for." I wrote it on a scrap of paper.

I looked at the piece of paper uncertainly. Then stuffed

it in my address book and went back to cleaning out the drawers.

***

A few days later, on a cold October afternoon, I was hurrying to the Union for a cup of coffee. With a crew of other workers I had just finished preparing the college grounds for winter, pruning, raking leaves and trimming. Despite my hooded sweatshirt over a turtleneck, cargo pants and work boots I was freezing.

I entered the Union, got my coffee and went over to a table near the windows. As I set my cup down I saw Professor Read come through the door. I wasn't sure if she saw me, so I sat down and tried to sip the hot coffee.

"Hello Julie. May I join you?" Professor Read stood next to my table holding a cup. She wore a heavy, expensive-looking red wool jacket and gray wool slacks.

"Yes, please." I pulled my cup back as if she needed more room for hers.

"You look frozen." She smiled. "Your cheeks are red."

"I've been working on fall cleanup for the grounds."

"No wonder the campus always looks so good. Do you work here?"

"No, I'm taking some horticulture classes."

She looked at me over her cup. "Getting your degree?"

"I have a degree and some graduate credits. I'm taking the classes because I've developed an interest in plants. Maybe I'll make a career change."

She sat back in her chair stretching out her long legs, and then crossing them. Pushing back a strand of her thick reddish hair she looked at me smiling faintly. I could easily understand why she was considered attractive and charismatic. Unable to think of something interesting to say I fiddled awkwardly with my coffee cup.

She said, "I think the orchestra is doing very well with

the Dvorak. It's a short symphony but with the Beethoven concerto our audience doesn't always appreciate a long program. What do you think, Julie?"

"Well, Professor, I feel this is one of the best groups I have played with."

She waved her hand. "You're not one of my students. Call me Vickie."

She leaned toward me. "We'll have to get together again, maybe for a drink." Then, examining her watch she announced. "I have to go." She stood up and looked down at me. "Don't forget to practice." Laughing, she walked away.

***

Back home I had just stepped out of a hot shower when the phone rang.

"I'm calling regarding your advertisement for the bedroom set." It was a pompous male voice. "What would you estimate its age?"

"I don't really know. It belonged to my aunt and she might have inherited it from her parents. That's just a guess."

"Will you be at home about six this evening? We could stop on the way to our rehearsal."

At six ten the doorbell rang. I opened it to a couple standing on the porch.

"James and Ellen Knight."

"Julie Burke." We shook hands.

As they entered the front foyer and passed through the French doors to the living room he looked around. "I don't remember this house being for sale."

"It wasn't. I'll show you the bedroom set."

As he looked up the open staircase to the second floor I examined him: a trim beard, styled hair and wearing a dark turtleneck sweater.

"The bedroom set is in here." I led the way to my aunt's bedroom.

"So this is your house?" The wife had a long scarf wound around her neck. She patted her dark, unruly permed hair. "We looked for a long time to find something of this style. We finally found a home about six blocks from here."

I could guess she was thinking how would I have the resources to own this home.

"This house belonged to my aunt. In here." I motioned to the bedroom set.

They both eagerly approached the pieces, pulling out drawers, running their hands over the wood surface and checking behind the chest and drawers.

He stood back and frowned. "How much are you asking?"

"Three hundred." Just then the phone rang and I went into the hall to answer it. Someone was calling about the bedroom set. "I have some people here now looking at it. If you want to give me your number I can call you after they leave and let you know if it's still available." This was loud enough for the Knights to hear.

When I went back in the room they were whispering together. There was a pause, they exchanged looks and he announced, "We'll take it. Will you be home Saturday morning? I have friends with a truck."

He wrote a check for a deposit then looked at the mantel clock. "We have to run. Green River Theater Guild rehearsal tonight."

She looked across the room and pointed to a chair. With a heavy carved wood frame it was upholstered in some faded floral material. "Is that chair for sale?"

I had never cared for the chair. "You can have the chair if your friends can help carry a library table down from a second-floor bedroom." I intended to use it as my desk.

"Yes, of course, we can do that Saturday."

Everyone was happy and they left.

***

I awoke in the early morning, three thirty by my clock radio. The dream had come again and this time I was trying to escape from the building as the fire alarm rang. My legs refused to move while everyone else hurried out leaving me behind. This, of course, had not happened, I had left with the rest of my co-workers. As I lay there I listened to the rain falling. It wasn't the torrential downpour of the night in the Rathskeller but a gentle, soothing patter on the roof. This was one of the reasons I liked sleeping on the second floor.

In my mind I went over my conversation with Vickie in the Union. It seemed awkward to call her that but I had heard others in the orchestra refer to her by that name. She was undoubtedly alluring but I thought there was another side to her. She was competitive and always got what she wanted. I fell asleep wondering what Vickie wanted now.

CHAPTER EIGHT

Professor Read—I still had trouble thinking of her as Vickie—stepped up onto the podium. "Before we tune I want to remind everyone of some upcoming dates. I know you all have been given a schedule but just in case some of you have misplaced yours…" She paused and looked around as nervous laughter came from some of the orchestra members.

"No rehearsal next week. It's the Thanksgiving vacation and the school is closed. The next Monday is our last regular rehearsal. Dress rehearsal is Friday night and the concert is Sunday, always the first Sunday in December.

If we schedule it any later the audience expects Christmas music. Any questions?"

A second violin player raised her hand. "Will the soloist be at the next rehearsal?"

"Oh yes, Monday night and the dress rehearsal. As you know she is the winner of the Youth Concerto Competition and quite talented. Also, Joanne's daughter will be here with her harp."

I blew air into my horn to keep it warm as I listened. Fascinating as Vickie was, I was eager to begin playing. Finally we started with the Dvorak so the trombones could leave afterward. When Lily played the lovely soft ascending passage to close the second movement, several of the orchestra members shuffled their feet. I joined them. This was the equivalent of clapping for a well-played passage by another member.

At the break I stood up and awkwardly looked around. Alan, who helped out in the percussion section when he wasn't conducting, came up behind us.

"Hi horns, sounding good." He stood there eagerly awaiting our attention. Tonight he was wearing a faded Brewers T-shirt, which was either from his thinner years or had shrunk in the wash.

"Thanks, Alan." Terri went off to talk to some other players and Karen followed her.

I thought this guy could be a pest. But then as he moved closer to Katy I was relieved to see them walk to the back of the room together. Whatever had happened with Amy two years ago, he appeared to have gotten over it.

I wandered out to the hall for a drink at the bubbler. As I lifted my head after drinking, Lily was standing behind me.

"Hello, Julie. Let me get a quick drink." She bent over, holding her hair back, then turned to face me. "Not only am I thirsty, I'm hungry. I had to meet with students this afternoon and didn't have time to eat, even though I don't like to eat too much before our rehearsal."

"I know. I usually eat something more when I get home later."

Lily removed a piece of lint from her sweater then looked up. "Would you be interested in stopping somewhere after the rehearsal?"

Was she really asking me to join her? "Oh yes, I would."

"Do you mind if we don't go to Dos Amigos? It will be full of orchestra members."

I knew what she meant. A lot of noise and orchestra shop talk. "What about Harry's Place? I'm sure they serve until at least ten." This was a bar and restaurant, popular with all ages, with good food and always busy. Several evenings I had passed by after rehearsal, seeing the crowd in the large windows overlooking the street and wishing I could stop. I never dreamed it would be with Lily.

"That sounds great. Can we meet there?"

Together we walked back to the stage where Vickie was already at her music stand turning the pages of the score, anxious to start rehearsing.

***

At Harry's Place all the tables in the front room were occupied and the bar was filled with people standing holding their drinks. The décor was very plain with no eye-catching paintings, posters or sports memorabilia on the walls. I accepted a table in the back room where it was quieter, telling the hostess another woman would be joining me. Before the waitress, or server, arrived at the table I saw the hostess point in my direction as Lily came across the room. A man at a nearby table watched her with obvious interest. He was the type I had imagined her to be married to, physically fit, distinguished-looking and well dressed. Oblivious to him she smiled and sat down, removing her leather gloves, coat and scarf. She looked so lovely; I was so happy and proud to be with her.

"Sorry I'm late, Julie. I was delayed going over some trill fingerings with the flute section." She grinned. "I guess I am the trill fingering expert."

We each ordered a glass of wine and a turkey sandwich. When our wine arrived Lily took a sip, then leaned back in her chair, tipped her head and looked at me.

"Do you have plans for Thanksgiving, Julie?"

"Not really. Just stay home, maybe watch some football." I waited for her to tell me her plans.

"That sounds relaxing. I'm flying to Seattle to visit my brother and his family."

"That should be fun."

She sighed. "Well, yes and no. We haven't seen each other in almost two years. He wanted me to come for Christmas but the airports are so crowded then and the weather is chancy. I kind of know what the holiday will be. He has three children, his wife's parents will be there and her sister who has three, maybe it's four, children. Also some of Phillip's friends usually drop in so I will see some of the football games. I'm looking forward to being with Phillip. Just more confusion than I'm used to."

She sat silently for a moment and then asked, "Aren't any of your friends getting together for Thanksgiving?"

"Probably, but I don't feel like driving to Milwaukee."

"I already have my reservation or…" Her voice trailed off.

Sitting across from her at the small table I was aware of her delicate hands and carefully manicured nails as she played with the stem of the wineglass. My own nails were clean and trimmed, but I could see my cuticles needed some attention.

"How are the classes coming?"

"I'm really enjoying them. Next semester I plan to take

a full load." Eager to share my newfound plant knowledge with her I offered, "The other day in one of my classes I learned something interesting."

Lily put an elbow on the table, rested her chin on her hand and gazed at me with a half smile."

"I'm not too technically inclined."

I laughed. "Not like that. You know the Dutch elm disease?"

"Oh yes. The street where I was brought up lost all their Dutch elms."

"There's no species called Dutch elm. The disease gets its name because of the contribution of Dutch women scientists who studied the disease."

"Really? Now that is interesting. I've always wanted to visit the Netherlands, especially Amsterdam."

I leaned forward eagerly. "You too? I would love to go there, especially in the spring when the tulip fields are in bloom."

We sat in silence for a few minutes. Perhaps Lily was imagining a trip to Amsterdam as I was. I looked up to see her stifling a yawn.

"I am sorry, Julie. I'm just tired from work, not the company." She smiled. "Never the company."

I signaled for the check. "Let's get out of here."

As we walked across the parking lot together I was acutely aware of her body next to me.

We approached our cars and Lily pulled on her leather gloves while I reached in my jacket pocket for my car key.

"I forgot to ask, what is concert dress for our orchestra?"

"Dark suits for the men with white shirts and dark ties. Long black skirt or slacks and black top for the women. Is this what your orchestra in Milwaukee wore?"

"Yes, except the men wore black bow ties."

Lily smiled. "We're not as formal up here."

I stalled, not wanting the evening to end. "I didn't ask. Are you flying out of Milwaukee?"

"First from Green Bay, then Milwaukee. A friend in my department has a daughter in Green Bay so she's driving there Wednesday to stay with her and coming back Sunday. It works out perfectly, she'll take me to the airport and pick me up."

"If anything happens and it doesn't work out let me know. I could drive you."

Lily put a gloved hand on my arm. "That is very kind of you, I appreciate it."

I didn't want her to take her hand away. What more could I say to keep her here? "Have a safe trip."

Why did I say that? I usually said something like "Have fun" or "Have a good time." Could it be I was worried about her flying across the country on a plane without adequate maintenance or flown by a pilot who had a couple of drinks before the flight? I had to stop watching the news.

Lily squeezed my arm and removed her hand. "Have a good Thanksgiving, Julie. I'll be thinking of you." She paused and then turned away.

As I drove home I was counting the days to our next rehearsal when I would see Lily again.

CHAPTER NINE

I walked into what formerly had been my aunt's bedroom and looked around. There wasn't much to see. The room was now bare except for the library table and some fluffy dull tan carpeting covering the floor.

I got a linoleum knife out of my tool drawer and, kneeling down, I pried up a piece of the carpet in a corner. As I suspected, underneath was a hardwood floor. Here was a project for the next week. Rip out the carpeting. It had hit me that I had another week ahead of me with no classes and no orchestra rehearsals. I did have a paper to write for one of my classes but I had already done most of the research.

I pulled open the drawer of the library table. My address book lay there. I opened it to the page where I had stuck the scrap with Thomas Gorman's phone number, impulsively picked it up, went to the phone and dialed the number.

On the third ring someone answered. "Yes, hello." A woman's voice sounding at least middle-aged.

"I'm calling the Thomas Gorman residence. My name is Julia Burke. I wonder if you are related to Laura Gorman?"

There was silence and then, cautiously, "My husband was Thomas Gorman, he's gone now. Why do you ask about Laura?"

"My aunt was Margaret Burke, she died about six months ago, and I found some pictures and references to Laura Gorman in her things. I know she wasn't at her funeral so I wondered if she..." I stopped. What should I say? Is she still alive? Is she dead?

"She was my husband's aunt. I don't know where she is. What did you say your aunt's name was?"

"Margaret Burke. She and Laura must have been good friends, they traveled together."

"I remember your aunt but Laura disappeared almost thirty years ago."

"Disappeared?"

She sighed. "I don't know what to say. One day she drove away and we never saw her again."

"Mrs. Gorman, if I were in Iron Mountain, say on Saturday, could I visit with you for just a short time?"

"You can call me June. I suppose I will be home Saturday. How about one in the afternoon?"

"That would be fine. I'll call when I get to town if I have trouble finding your house."

She gave me her address and I gave her my phone number in case her plans changed.

When I hung up I realized that for who knew what reason I had committed myself to a trip to Iron Mountain.

***

Wednesday morning, the day before Thanksgiving, I drove over to the supermarket for snacks to eat during the football games. The parking lot was jammed as cars backed out of their spots, narrowly missing the cars parked behind them, and frenzied people hurried to their cars pushing overflowing carts while trying to avoid being run over. I always parked as far from the entrance as I could so even today I was able to find a spot.

I bought several kinds of cheese, fresh shrimp, a loaf of French bread and sliced turkey breast, my one gesture to the holiday. Then I waited in a long checkout line for what seemed like forever. I let my mind wander. Lily would be at the airport leaving today. I had to stop thinking about her. One of these days I would discover an old boyfriend had come to town and that would be the end of it. End of what? We'd only had a drink together a couple of times.

When I got home and had everything put away I thought about my upcoming trip. Since I had never been to Iron Mountain I had no idea how long the trip would take so I got out a road map. Laying the map out on the kitchen table I traced the route with my finger and estimated it would take about two hours.

Saturday morning I was up early. I didn't plan to stay overnight but just in case, I threw a few things including a book on Japanese gardens into an overnight bag. I grabbed my heavy parka from the closet and looked out at the gray sky wondering what Lily was doing in Seattle.

For the first hour I drove through desolate-looking small towns. It was too late for fishing season and too early for snowmobiling. Some of the shops had For Sale signs in their windows. The chain supermarkets and Walmart had moved business to the outskirts leaving behind abandoned downtowns.

I drove through huge expanses of pines, and snowflakes begin swirling, light at first, then heavier until I had to turn on my headlights as passing cars threw sheets of snow onto my windshield.

What I estimated should have taken two hours was going on three when I saw the sign announcing Iron Mountain.

At a gas station just inside the city limits I filled up and got myself a sturdy snowbrush with a scraper on one end, and a box of chocolates done up for the coming holiday season with a big red bow. This would be a gift for June Gorman.

I took my purchases to the counter where two young girls were working and pulled the piece of paper with June Gorman's address from my pocket.

"Could you tell me how to find this address?"

The girl in a Packers sweatshirt, her brown hair pulled behind her ears, examined the paper. The other girl, who wore a fleece jacket with the name of the station on it, leaned over to see it and gave me the directions.

I thanked them and went out to use my new snowbrush on the back window, which was already covered with snow. As I drove slowly through town I saw a motel and across from it a supper club. I turned into the motel parking lot. Any thought of driving back home this afternoon was gone.

An older woman with thick glasses and wearing a heavy wool ski sweater was behind the desk talking on the telephone. I approached and waited until she hung up.

"Can I help you?" She arranged some papers in front of her.

"I'd like a room for tonight."

She looked up. "This is the holiday weekend you know."

"I didn't plan to stay overnight, but now with this weather…"

She looked out the window. "A little early this year. You're lucky. Someone just checked out but the room isn't ready yet. Probably two hours."

"That's fine. I have some business to take care of." I handed her my credit card.

After the room had been arranged I went out to the Jeep and once again used the new snowbrush. Now the snow was heavy and steady, rapidly covering everything. I found the street where June lived and drove slowly, peering at the house numbers until I found hers. An artificial wreath hung on June's front door and painted plywood cutouts of a Santa and a snowman were propped up on her front lawn. The falling snow had already left little piles of snow on the thin edges of the plywood. Her one-story house was covered in pale yellow aluminum siding and through the front windows I could see plastic on the inside to help keep out the cold air.

Clutching my box of chocolates I rang the doorbell. I could hear it buzz inside and then the door opened so quickly that I suspected June Gorman had been watching for me out the window.

"So you made it, even in this weather. Come in." June held the door open.

I stepped in and stomped my feet on a soiled remnant of carpet just inside the door. "Let me take my shoes off."

"No, it's all right, you can wipe your feet here. Come in."

June was wearing one of those Christmas sweatshirts decorated with sparkle and a jolly snowman with World's Greatest Aunt emblazoned under him. Her graying brown hair had recently been permed, probably for the

Thanksgiving holiday and her pleasant wrinkled face had a minimum of makeup.

As I handed her the box of chocolates she exclaimed, "Oh, what a treat, and such a pretty ribbon. Here, let me take your jacket." She laid it on an empty chair. "I hope it's not too cold in here for you. With the price of fuel oil I keep it turned down."

I thought guiltily of all the times in my house when I jacked up the thermostat at the least hint of a chill in the air. Besides the chocolates I carried the envelope with the pictures of my aunt and Laura Gorman.

"Sit here." June motioned toward a lounge chair covered in green imitation leather. On a table next to it was a plate of cookies. The chair was unexpectedly cold when I sat down.

June sat in a floral overstuffed chair opposite me. "Now tell me about your aunt."

I explained that after she died I had found several photos and references to Laura Gorman. I didn't mention the letters.

June lit a cigarette with a brightly colored disposable lighter. "Laura was a history teacher at the high school here."

"My aunt was a high school history teacher too. Maybe they met at a course or workshop."

"Could be." She blew a puff of smoke into the room. "Say, does this bother you that I smoke?"

"No, of course not." How could I say it had killed my mother?

"Have a cookie." June pointed to the plate. "Made them this morning."

"Thanks." I picked up a star with white icing and popped it in my mouth. Very tasty. I realized I hadn't eaten since my meager breakfast. I picked up another star, avoiding a bell with one of those metallic silver beads for the clapper. Hard on the teeth.

I opened the manila envelope and removed the pictures of Laura and my aunt. "Is this your aunt Laura?"

June reached for them. "Oh yes, she was my husband's aunt but we got along real good. A smart lady." She picked up a picture from the end table next to her. "I found this after you called. This is Laura when she was younger."

It was unmistakably Laura Gorman. Her identity now established, I decided to get to the story. "What exactly happened to her?"

June picked up her cigarette, took a deep drag and put the cigarette back in the yellow ceramic ashtray on the table next to her. I picked up another cookie, avoiding the bell.

"She left alone in her car, we thought it was probably for grocery shopping in the late afternoon. She never came home. I do remember it was raining that day..."

I let June continue.

"They searched everywhere and not just here in Michigan. Tom and I always wondered if she had met someone we didn't know about and took off with him. But she didn't take any money out of her bank account, and so then we thought well maybe she got sick or something happened before she could."

"I'm sure my aunt was upset. They were close friends."

"Yes, I remember your aunt came up here. She couldn't understand what had happened to Laura. She was hard on the police but they did everything they could."

June crushed out her cigarette and lit another. "After a certain period of time, I can't remember how long, we sold her house. It was sad getting rid of her belongings. We kept hoping, but then we gave up." She stood up and went to the window. "Pretty bad out there. I hope you aren't driving home. I can put you up here."

"Thanks so much but when I saw all the snow I got a room in a motel here in town."

There wasn't much more to say about Laura Gorman. I

stood up. "You have my address and phone number. Please let me know if you learn anything more."

June shook her head. "I'm afraid not after all these years."

We said goodbye and I went out, brushed the snow off the Jeep and drove away as June stood in the door waving to me. I liked her and intended to keep in touch with her.

At the motel my room was ready and while I waited for my room key I asked about the restaurant across the street, "What time does that place open?"

The desk clerk put the room card in a little folder and slapped it on the counter. "Second floor, room two twelve. The Pine Tree? Four thirty."

I glanced up at the clock over the desk. Three thirty.

"We have coffee and doughnuts in the lobby in the morning. Eight to eleven on Sunday."

My room was clean and utilitarian with a view of the parking lot. I removed the few items from my bag and stretched out on the bed with my book.

I woke up disoriented in the dark room. I had fallen asleep and now it was almost seven o'clock. Looking out the window I was dismayed to see the snow falling as heavily as earlier and my Jeep totally covered. I put on my parka and went down to the deserted lobby. The clerk was nowhere in sight. She was probably in the back room watching television.

I crossed the street to the Pine Tree Supper Club. The bar, facing a full-length mirror, was hung with imitation evergreen swags and surprisingly full of customers despite the weather. By now I was starving so I bypassed the bar to be led to a table. A waitress in a black skirt and top covered with a frilly white apron approached me, pen poised over a pad ready to take my order.

"I'll have a glass of chardonnay and I need a few minutes here." I indicated the menu, which was the usual supper club fare such as steak, chops and lobster. I decided the baked chicken was the best bet. It sounded like comfort food. Just what I needed tonight.

After my meal I trudged back across to the motel with two wet feet. Running shoes weren't the best choice for snow. In my room I propped my wet shoes against the heater hoping they would be dry by morning. After flipping around the few television channels I turned off the TV and finally fell asleep.

In the morning I awoke to the sound of a snowplow scraping the parking lot. The snow had stopped sometime during the night but the day was gray and overcast.

When I checked out the desk clerk glanced out the window and gloomily predicted, "Lucky you're leaving today. More snow coming tonight."

The snow held off on the journey home and as I came closer to Green River I noticed less and less snow until I arrived home to find it hadn't snowed there at all. The whole trip, especially the story of Laura Gorman's disappearance, took on a surreal aspect as if it had all been another one of my bad dreams.

CHAPTER TEN

Alan stepped up on the podium in Stofer Concert Hall in the Fine Arts Building, smiling broadly at us. It was three o'clock on the first Sunday in December and our concert was underway. Although the hall had a capacity of seven hundred, Terri told me it was rarely more than half filled when we performed. Our audience appeared to consist of the usual devoted community music lovers and friends and family of the musicians. This afternoon, the parents, relatives and classmates of our soloist made up a large contingent sitting as near the front of the hall as possible while visiting and chatting with one another.

Alan had arrived in the Fine Arts Building wearing a faded old Packers sweatshirt while carrying his tuxedo jacket on a hanger. Now, as he raised his arms to begin conducting I noticed the jacket was too tight across his chest. Probably another wardrobe item from his slimmer days.

Terri leaned over and whispered to me, "Vickie always lets him conduct one number, usually the overture."

We raised our horns. By now everyone was familiar enough with the "Rosamunde Overture" that we could have played it without Alan.

The overture ended and Alan took his bows to warm applause. The piano was rolled into place and the trombones left the stage. We waited in silence and then Vickie strode onto the stage to applause, preceded by our soloist, Jenny Kim. Vickie looked elegant in flowing black slacks and a black silk long-sleeved blouse. The soloist, a high school senior, was wearing a rose taffeta gown. She adjusted her bench, looked up at Vickie and then we launched into the first movement of the Beethoven Piano Concerto No. 1.

Somewhere in the Largo second movement I was counting eleven bars rest when I sensed something was wrong. Vickie rapidly turned a page of her score and mouthed what looked like "letter D," firmly giving the beat and making sure all of the strings had her attention. A few of the players had dropped out in confusion but finally regrouped and went on.

At the end of the movement Vickie took a little longer than usual to begin the Rondo, smiling encouragement to the orchestra and soloist. The concerto ended without further incident and the audience stood and applauded loudly for our soloist who shyly took several bows and accepted the bouquet brought onstage for her. Vickie motioned for the orchestra to stand and it was time for the intermission.

Out in the hall offstage the players milled around discussing what had happened, some of them still bewildered.

"What was that all about in the second movement?" The tall clarinet player with the frizzy hair was shaking her head.

One of the first violins answered her. "The soloist must have had a memory lapse because she skipped a whole section. Luckily Vickie saved the day." Several heads nodded in agreement.

Down the hall Lily was talking to some other woodwind players. Since Thanksgiving I hadn't had much opportunity to talk with her. She had said goodbye to me and left the Monday rehearsal as soon as it was over, and on Friday our dress rehearsal had lasted so long everyone just wanted to get out and go home afterward.

I had anxiously looked forward to this concert, not only for the chance to perform, but to be with Lily again. Last night in bed I had thought of Lily, but this time my thoughts were sensual as I imagined holding her with my lips pressed against her body. I felt a shiver as my body responded and I rolled over burying my face in the pillow imagining it was Lily's hair and throat I was kissing. Exhausted, I fell asleep with no dreams of the fire.

Seeing me looking over she smiled and waved to me but the intermission had ended and we filed back onstage for the Dvorak Symphony No. 4.

This was the piece we all looked forward to playing and I was relieved not to be playing first horn. I'd had bouts with performance anxiety in the past and although I always came through, it took its toll.

The Dvorak went well under Vickie's capable direction, ending about forty minutes later, short enough to keep the attention of most of our audience. Vickie pointed to the individual sections to stand for cheers and applause. We horns had our turn first and then it was all over.

After the concert there was a tradition of holding a reception with tables set up in the lobby offering wine and punch. After putting my horn away I went to the lobby. A crowd surrounded Vickie and further away a smaller group gathered around Alan who was beaming and explaining something as he gestured with his hands. I noticed he had unbuttoned his tight jacket. I turned away and walked over to the table, took a small plastic glass of wine and then looked up to see Lily standing next to me. Remembering my fantasy of the night before, I blushed. The feelings were still with me.

She reached for a glass of wine and then we moved away from the crowd at the table to a corner of the room where we had some privacy.

"What did you think of the soloist skipping a section in the second movement?"

Lily smiled at me over her glass. "We flutes didn't know what happened because we don't play in that movement but I could sense something was amiss."

"She seemed fine in the rehearsals."

"Probably not used to performing in front of such a large audience, although I don't think they noticed anything wrong."

"Vickie pulled us through."

"Yes." We stood in silence. "Are you going away for Christmas, Julie?"

"My friends in Milwaukee invited me down there but I told them I would come for New Year's. This year I want to spend Christmas in my house. For the last few years my aunt just had a tabletop artificial tree but I found a big tree stand and box of old ornaments in the basement. I'm going to have a real tree."

"What kind of house is it?"

"A Queen Anne. Not a huge one but it does have a big porch, bay windows and four bedrooms on the second floor. I tried to find some books about Queen Anne homes at the library but they didn't have much."

I took another sip of the wine. It was a little on the sweet side. "What are you doing for Christmas?"

"On Christmas Day our department chairman, Professor Fox, and his wife have an open house. It's very nice, I've gone the last two years."

"What about Christmas Eve?"

"I have no plans."

Should I ask her? Why not? "Since you don't have any plans would you like to come over and see my house?" That sounded like I was showing off. "I mean, spend Christmas Eve with me."

"That would be wonderful, and I am anxious to see your house."

As I looked at her I thought what a lovely smile she had and wondered if all these people surrounding us realized how attractive she was. She wore a long black skirt and her top was some soft material that showed off her breasts although I was sure it wasn't intentional.

I panicked when I remembered my lack of culinary skills. "Do you like Chinese food?"

"Yes." She laughed. "Doesn't everyone?"

"Would you be offended if I had Chinese food for dinner? I'm not a great cook."

"I would like that."

"Anything in particular that you like?"

"No, you decide. What time should I come?"

"Is five all right? Is it too early or too late?"

"Just right." Lily opened a small purse hanging on her shoulder and took out a pen. "Can you give me your address?"

I dictated my address and phone number, which she wrote on her cocktail napkin. I didn't ask for her phone number. It was in the telephone book. I knew because I had looked.

"What are you two plotting?" Vickie was standing next to us laughing. She took Lily by the arm. "Lily, come with me. I want you to meet someone."

A faint look of annoyance crossed Lily's face. I nodded slightly and smiled.

"Did Alan invite you to his party?"

I turned to see Terri standing behind me. "No, what party?"

Terri took a drink of her punch. "At the Mexican restaurant. I heard him ask your friend Lily. She's your friend isn't she?"

"Yes, she is."

"She told him she had some previous plans. Alan thinks he's quite the ladies' man lately."

"I thought he was interested in Katy."

"Yes, but I think he's looking around too. See you." Terri headed to the table for more punch.

One thing I knew was that Lily would not want anything to do with Alan, and I doubted if she had any plans for later. I finished my wine and discarded the plastic glass in the garbage can next to the table.

"Had enough?" Lily had come up behind me.

I grinned at her. "I heard you were invited to Alan's party."

She rolled her eyes. "Oh please, Julie. How about going to the Italian Villa? Have you ever been there?"

"No, but it sounds great if you recommend it."

She had that twinkle in her eye, which I had seen before and loved. I picked up my horn case. "Get your coat, let's go."

CHAPTER ELEVEN

I hurried down the walk from the Birmingham Science Building on the campus. My classes had ended for the semester but I had come over to pick up a completed laboratory project. The December days were growing increasingly colder and so much shorter. Today it was twenty-nine degrees and at four in the afternoon the light was already fading.

"Julie." Someone called my name and I turned to see Professor Read, Vickie as I now was trying to think of her, waving to me. I waited as she caught up with me.

"Why are you here on campus? You should be out Christmas shopping." She laughed and fell in step with me.

"I don't have much shopping to do. I was here to pick up a project." There weren't many presents for me to buy, only something to take to Ginger and Cindy and a present to have under the tree on Christmas Eve for Lily. I had been agonizing over this, not wanting to get anything too personal.

"I'm done for the day. Let's have a drink together." Vickie looked at me sideways.

"Okay, but I'm not sure if the Rathskeller is open."

She made a face. "No, not that place. I like Tosca. Do you know where it is?"

"Yes, I think so. Is it on Ohio Street?"

"That's it. I have to get my car from the faculty lot. See you there."

Tosca was a restaurant and cocktail lounge a few miles away. Far enough to be off campus and not patronized by the students. I had never been there but had the impression it catered to the steak-and-martini crowd.

I had a long walk to the student parking lot, and then had to scrape some frost from my windows so that when I walked into Tosca Vickie was already seated at a small table in the bar. She waved to me although it would have been hard to miss her. She was wearing a short tweed jacket over a maroon silk blouse open at the neck. The blouse picked up the highlights of her chestnut hair, which was down and flowing over her shoulders. I slid onto the high-backed chair at one of those elevated tables designed to give the impression you are sitting at the bar.

I looked around. Dim lighting, lots of mirrors, dramatic opera posters on the walls and orchestral arrangements of opera arias playing softly in the background. The bar was already crowded with what looked like businessmen and groups of women who had just ended an afternoon of shopping.

A waiter approached our table and laid down two cocktail napkins. He was wearing a long-sleeved white shirt, unbuttoned at the neck, with a black leather vest over it. His dark hair was freshly combed, and I detected the heavy scent of some men's cologne.

"Hello Dr. Read. Ready for Christmas?"

"Of course not, Tony. I'll have a martini; you know how I like it. Make it two."

I started to protest. "I'm not sure if—"

Vickie waved her hand. "They are the best here. You'll love it."

The few times I had tried a martini it had literally made me shudder when I drank it. Best not to protest, I thought.

Tony brought the martinis and a dish of nuts, which he placed between us. "Enjoy."

We picked up our drinks and, true to my previous experience, a sip of the martini again sent tremors through me. When I looked up Vickie was setting her drink down and a sizable amount was gone. She sighed. "Tony certainly makes the best."

One of the post-shopping trip women hovered next to our table. "Vickie! How I loved the concert." Slim, with a blond pageboy, perfect makeup and an expensive suit, she was holding a glass of wine. I wanted to exchange our drinks.

She added, "I'm so looking forward to the next concert in the spring. I heard you have something special planned."

There was a dramatic pause as Vickie lifted her martini, took a sip and set it carefully down. "Marty, that *will* be a special concert."

Marty examined her jewel-encrusted watch. "I can't wait. See you at the next meeting, Vickie." She went back to join her friends.

"On the community orchestra board." Vickie watched her leave.

"What are we playing for the next concert?" I tried another sip of my drink.

"The Kalinnikov Symphony No. 1. Almost never performed. A lovely piece. I expect we will have quite a large audience; many will come just to hear it performed live." She peered at me over her glass. "Are you familiar with it?"

"No, I'm not."

"Beautiful horn parts. Get the CD, I think there's only one readily available recording, or Alan can make a tape for you."

I was determined to order the CD along with one I was thinking of giving Lily for Christmas.

Vickie was signaling Tony for another drink. I still had half of mine sitting in front of me. I picked it up and unsuccessfully attempted another sip.

"Are we having a soloist on the next concert?"

"Oh yes, this one is a clarinet player, a college student. Hopefully he's not prone to memory problems. The Weber Concertino for Clarinet. A nice short piece." She shifted in her chair and crossed her legs. "Enough talk of the orchestra."

Vickie's drink arrived, and I desperately tried to think of a new subject but she was ahead of me.

"Do you like it here or do you think you will be moving back to Milwaukee?"

"I'm not going back. This is my home now."

Vickie picked up her fresh drink and peered at it. "Spending Christmas here?"

"Yes, I am."

"Not me. I'm going to New York, upstate that is. I have a friend, well friends there. I am from that area."

I took another sip, already feeling a little out of it. What could I talk about? Maybe I could learn something about Amy.

"I guess I told you I played with Amy Leland when I lived in Milwaukee."

Vickie made an expression of displeasure. "Were you close friends?"

"No, I only played with her in the orchestra."

"Just as well. She was a self-centered, troubled woman."

What could I say? I pushed my glass around on the cocktail napkin. "I guess she was a pretty good horn player."

Vickie picked up a nut and leaned forward. "Not that great. That idiot Alan gave her the first chair because he had the hots for her. I mean, Marcy wasn't so wonderful but she was at least dependable. But I couldn't overturn his decision."

She leaned back and popped the nut into her mouth. "You know, I think you four horns playing together are the best group we've had since I've been here."

"Thank you, we get along pretty well."

Vickie ignored me and picked up her drink, drained it and motioned to Tony. Looking across the room into space she slowly shook her head. "Amy was trouble, I should have known. Those things she said about me that night. It was pretty bad. Everything went wrong."

I tried to sip the remainder of my martini. What was she talking about? Maybe they'd had a confrontation about Amy's playing.

Tony delivered Vickie's martini. She motioned toward my glass. "Bring my friend another. Tony, this is Julie, one of my musicians."

Tony dipped his head. "Nice to meet you. Dr. Read is the best."

He left and Vickie looked at me. "Lovely sweater, is it cashmere?"

"Yes, it is." This was one of my few expensive clothing purchases after receiving my inheritance.

"Blue. Matches your eyes." She looked around the

bar then back at me. "What in the world do you do for entertainment here? You're not exactly a new young college student. I would imagine you're not having any problems with your classes. Probably got all A's."

That was true. "I'm finding horticulture interesting and I do enjoy the classes. I'm also working on my house. You know, renovating and redecorating, that kind of thing."

Tony delivered my drink with a fresh cocktail napkin.

Vickie picked up a nut. "I'd like to see it. Would you invite me sometime?" She put the nut in her mouth. "Are you friends with Lily?"

For some reason I was wary of her question. "Yes, but I don't know her very well, just from our orchestra rehearsals." Maybe I didn't want to expose her to Vickie's scrutiny.

"I thought I saw you two talking and leaving together after rehearsals."

"Probably with a group from the orchestra." I went back to the original question. "I would be happy to have you over to see my house."

"Yes, I'll come sometime. What's up for New Year's?"

"I'm going to Milwaukee to be with some friends."

"Do you go there often?"

I tentatively sipped the new drink. "No, not since August."

"They must miss you. Any special friend?"

"No, we just all worked together, and I lived in an apartment complex with some of them. You know, near work."

Vickie lifted her glass and examined it. "I live far enough from the campus to be away from the students but still a comfortable commute."

She finished her drink and signaled to Tony for the check, then looked at me and smiled. "You have to learn to appreciate a martini. We'll see about the house visit."

I protested but she insisted on paying the check and

we walked out to the parking lot. Vickie was driving a Lincoln Navigator and appeared amused that I was driving a Wrangler.

"Julie, I guess you're an outdoor girl." She waved, opened her door, got in and drove away.

I had intended to pick up a Christmas tree this afternoon but instead drove straight home. Tired, hungry and heavy-headed from the martinis, I deposited the lab project in my empty office, opened a can of chicken noodle soup and made half of a toasted cheese sandwich. After I ate I got ready for bed and went up to my bedroom to read but I soon fell asleep with troubled dreams. This time Vickie was urging me to go back in the burning laboratory building to help my dying co-workers.

CHAPTER TWELVE

Two days after my afternoon with Vickie I was at the garden center to buy my tree. I strolled between the rows of Christmas trees, inspecting them and taking in their pine scent.

"Hey, Julie."

I turned around to see Denise from my Fungi horticulture course. As older students we had gravitated toward each other. I knew she worked at a garden center so here she was, outside with the Christmas trees.

"Hi Denise, I'm looking for a tree that's taller than I am, otherwise I'm not sure what kind."

Denise was wearing a down jacket on top of a hooded sweatshirt, its hood pulled over medium-length brown hair with a sprinkling of gray, which lent a dramatic appearance to her otherwise slim, youthful, look.

She pointed to a well-shaped fat tree. "Here, these are Scotch pine, very popular now. Long needle retention."

I pointed to a tree further down the row. "What about that kind?"

"Balsam fir. The traditional Christmas tree."

"That's what I want."

Denise walked down the row and picked up a tree that appeared to be just right. She turned it around and we agreed this was the one.

"I'll go cut off the bottom of the trunk." She carried the tree over to where a chain saw lay, fired it up and began cutting.

While she was busy I looked at a display of wreaths. I vaguely remembered my aunt always having a large one hanging at a certain place at the front of the house on the porch. The nail might even be there.

Denise, who was wearing heavy leather gloves, carried the tree to my Jeep. We put it inside with the wreath on a large tarp I'd brought along to catch the needles. When it was secured she pulled up the sleeve of her jacket to look at her watch.

"I'm done in a half hour. Care to meet me for a drink?"

"I have another errand to take care of. That would be fine."

"How about the Golden Lantern? Two blocks south of downtown on Spring Street."

This was the area of downtown that was deteriorating. I agreed, but wondered why she wanted to meet there.

My errand was to go to a florist shop downtown and order a poinsettia plant for June Gorman.

The clerk in the florist shop was an older woman

wearing a denim jacket embroidered with large snowflakes. She approached me with a forced smile. "Can I help you?"

"I want to send a poinsettia to Iron Mountain, Michigan. Something nice."

We looked at the selections together; I picked the largest one, and then paid with my credit card.

When I pulled up in front of the Golden Lantern I sat in the Jeep. The bar's front windows were covered with shutters halfway up and curtains covered the rest. A neon outline of a golden lantern hung in a front window and a lighted beer sign above the door announced Golden Lantern. It was a few minutes after five but I always felt awkward entering a bar or restaurant alone. Just as I had finally decided to go in I saw Denise pull up in an older, small pickup truck. I got out and waited for her.

"Hey, just in time." She waved and we entered the bar together.

I was surprised the bar was so busy this early. But then I thought Christmas was less than two weeks away and a lot of people were already on vacation.

"Denise baby, over here." Two women at a table near the bar waved at her.

We joined them and Denise introduced them but I had trouble catching their names in the noisy, smoky place. We removed our jackets and hung them over the backs of our chairs. Denise was no longer wearing her sweatshirt but had on a tight black and white striped sweater. I noticed she had several rings on each hand and two gold chains laden with various pendants and charms around her neck. A waitress, server that is, came over and slapped two beer coasters on the table. I looked up to see a young woman with spiky black hair and a tattoo on her forearm. It was a red rose on a long stem complete with thorns and several leaves. Maybe she was a horticulture student.

Denise ordered a Miller Lite, and I ordered a Heineken. When the beers arrived I asked for a glass.

Tattoo came back and plunked it on the table. I noticed no one else had a glass. Denise picked up her bottle and took a swig. She looked at her friends and motioned toward me.

"Julie and I are in the horticulture program together at Northbrook." The two women nodded, looking impressed.

Denise leaned toward me. "How do you like the program?"

"I really enjoy it. Next semester I'm taking a full load of courses."

Denise took another drink. "I wish I could but I just can't afford it. I have to work full time. I'm so sick of that garden center. My supervisor is such a chauvinist, and they don't even know how to run the place decently."

I was embarrassed that I had said I would be taking so many classes and wasn't sure what to say. "I imagine the experience working there is helpful."

Denise made a face. Just then the two women at our table got up and went over to a small dance floor in the back room next to the pool table. I looked over at the bar, all women, and then I understood. It seemed the city of Green River might have its own place in the directory of gay and lesbian bars.

I wondered if this might be an opportunity to learn something about Amy. I sipped my beer and looked at Denise. "Someone I knew in Milwaukee moved up here. I wonder if you knew her? Amy Leland."

Denise was in the process of lifting her beer bottle but set it down abruptly. "She was a friend of yours?"

I saw the same look on her face as the others when I had asked about Amy. What was it? Certainly not a look of pleasure. "No, we played in a musical group together. I really didn't know her very well."

Denise picked up her bottle again. "Amy moved up here to be with Mary. There was trouble from the beginning. Amy argued with her all the time. Mary had a good job but I think Amy used her. One night Amy was abusive to Mary and maybe not just verbally. Mary wouldn't talk about it but she asked Amy to move out. We were all glad because Mary is a nice person and didn't deserve that. I think Amy was fooling around with someone else because after that she never came back here to the bar. I guess it was with a woman who wouldn't want to be seen in here."

Denise took another drink. "Then Amy disappeared. We thought she took off with someone." She signaled for another beer and laughed. "Whoever that was, we all felt sorry for her."

She looked around the bar and I could tell Denise had had enough of talking about Amy. "Are you hungry? The pizza here is pretty good."

I ordered another beer along with Denise. "Pizza sounds great."

Just then Denise looked up toward the door with an eager expression on her face. "Here comes Mary." In a lower voice she added. "Don't mention Amy."

Denise raised her arm, the woman came over to our table, Denise stood up and they hugged.

"Mary, this is Julie. We were in a horticulture class together."

"Hi Julie." Mary put out her hand then removed her black wool coat and red scarf. She was stylishly dressed in gray wool slacks, heels and a red mock turtleneck sweater. As she sat down Denise explained proudly. "Mary works at City Hall in the office."

"Nice to meet you, Mary. I was just there to pay my property taxes."

Mary placed her purse on the table and rolled her eyes. "Worst time of the year. Everyone complains about their taxes." She ran a hand over her short frosted hair then turned to Denise. "I'm glad you finally got out of work on time tonight."

Denise beamed. "We were just thinking about ordering a pizza. Want to join us?"

"Sounds great. I don't feel like cooking when I get home."

As Denise and Mary exchanged complaints about their jobs I looked around the bar thinking that a few years ago I would have been thrilled to discover a women's bar here in Green River. Now I really didn't care. Maybe it was just the mood I was in tonight.

The pizzas arrived and as is often the case, conversation dwindled while we ate. When we were finished and the check had arrived I put down enough bills to cover the tip and stood up. "I better get going. This is on me."

"Thanks. See you next semester, Julie." Denise raised her bottle in a salute.

Mary added, "Nice meeting you, hope to see you again."

I didn't feel guilty about leaving Denise, she seemed happy to be with Mary and I hoped something worked out for them. They both deserved someone better than Amy.

Driving home with my newly acquired tree, I thought about what Denise had told me about Amy. I had never found Amy attractive. She probably was, with shoulder-length blond hair, brown eyes like her sister Beth, and a good body. I had never cared for her abrasive personality and she was what my aunt would have described as "forward." But evidently she had charmed several people during her brief stay in Green River.

CHAPTER THIRTEEN

I turned off the room lights and examined the Christmas tree. Decorated with three strings of tiny white lights and all of my aunt's precious old ornaments, it was lovely. The tree fit perfectly into the sturdy stand I found in the basement, and I had arranged a round plaid tablecloth underneath as a tree skirt.

My Christmas shopping was done. A pizza oven and a large box of assorted cheese and sausage for Ginger and Cindy, and when I had the music store order the Kalinnikov recording I also ordered a CD of the Bach *Concertos for Flute and Strings* played by Jean Pierre Rampal for Lily. Two days earlier I had received a Christmas card from June Gorman thanking me for the beautiful poinsettia plant and wishing me a blessed holiday.

The dining room table was set with my aunt's best china and silver. Two taper candles in silver holders were on the table ready to be lit and I had a fire blazing in the fireplace.

Now, I was nervous. What if Lily had received a better invitation for Christmas Eve and was afraid of hurting my feelings by canceling our evening and was only coming here reluctantly?

At five o'clock the doorbell chimed. I hurried to open it. Lily stood there smiling, wearing a long black wool coat with a soft gray scarf and carrying two packages.

I hung up her coat and scarf in the front hall closet. Lily held out her packages.

"Some wine for us and something for you to put under your tree."

Speechless, I led her to the living room and placed her package under the tree next to my present for her.

"Julie, this tree is beautiful." She began examining the ornaments.

"These ornaments are so unusual. Look at the pickle, those Santas and the birds. They must be very old." Then she looked around her at the living room. "What a handsome room and I love the fireplace."

She was lovely in a dark green sweater of some soft material, maybe cashmere, and black wool slacks. I went over to a corner near the bay windows and turned back to look at her.

"Do you play the piano?" I asked her.

"Yes, but I don't have much opportunity now."

"I don't know how. Someday I would like to learn but I think a baby grand would fit perfectly here. I'm thinking of getting one."

"Julie, a baby grand is very expensive, even a used one."

I had already priced them but made no comment. "Would you like to see the upstairs?"

We climbed the stairs and I showed her the four bedrooms, saving mine for last. After looking at the others we stood in the doorway of my bedroom and peered in. I had dusted, vacuumed, and arranged everything neatly.

Lily looked around her. "You know, what I love is that each bedroom is in a corner of the house so it has windows on two walls."

"In the summer it can get quite warm up here so I'm thinking of getting air-conditioning installed in the spring. Maybe a new furnace too."

Lily stepped into my bedroom and glanced up. "Perhaps a ceiling fan would help in the summer. They aren't too expensive."

She was standing near my bed and I had a fleeting image of me pulling her down onto my bed, holding her in my arms. I pushed the thought away as we walked out into the hall. I pointed to a door at the end of the hallway.

"Those stairs lead to the third floor. There are windows but it's not finished off, just an attic."

Downstairs I showed her what was to be my office. "My aunt used this room as her bedroom. I sold the bedroom set to some couple who seemed to be a big deal in the Theater Guild. The Knights."

Lily laughed. "I know who you mean. They always manage to have their picture in the paper. Slightly pretentious."

"I want to make it into an office or den. I tore out the carpeting and found the floor underneath was hardwood so I cleaned it but now I can't decide if I should leave that older look or have it professionally sanded and refinished."

I pointed to the wall without windows. "I want to have bookshelves built on that wall, but have to find someone to do it."

Lily looked at the wall and thought for a moment. "I

wonder if you could buy some ready-made bookshelves. They come in different kinds of wood and sizes. That is, if you can't find someone to build them."

As we walked back to the living room Lily was silent and seemed uncomfortable. Suddenly I understood that my talk of air-conditioning, refinishing floors, building bookcases and buying a piano was upsetting Lily because she thought I didn't have any money. Of course she knew I had inherited the house but there was the associated expense of upkeep and property taxes and here I was with no job and tuition expenses.

I wondered if it would be boasting to tell her that besides the house I had inherited over a million dollars. Instead, I motioned for us to sit down on the couch. I leaned forward and nervously took a deep breath.

"Lily, my aunt was a high school history teacher but years ago she realized that on a teacher's salary she could never afford the things she wanted, a house and travel. Some friends recommended a stockbroker they knew and my aunt began investing in the stock market, as much as she could afford each month. She wasn't afraid to take risks and soon she was able to buy this house. She never stopped investing." I felt as if I was delivering a lecture but continued. "Anyway, she didn't just leave me this house. She left me an enormous amount of money. Financially, I am quite well off."

I nervously waited for Lily's reply. After a few moments she looked over at me.

"Julie, I am so happy for you." Then she smiled mischievously. "You know, I think you should get that baby grand piano."

We laughed together. "Should we have dinner now?"

"That would be wonderful. I can't wait for Chinese food."

While I heated the dishes in the microwave I asked Lily to light the candles on the table.

I came to the doorway and watched as the flickering candles illuminated her dark hair falling in her face and her fine profile. "What do you think? Tea with our meal and the wine afterward?"

Lily looked up. "I think that would be a good idea."

I put on a CD of *The Messiah*. "I love this. I have three versions. A period orchestra playing on authentic instruments, the Chicago Symphony version with one hundred singers and a CD of the London Symphony playing excerpts using forty-eight voices."

"Which is this?" Lily asked, laughing.

"The excerpts." In the soft candlelight I looked over at Lily and could hardly eat. Why did this beautiful woman want to spend Christmas Eve at my house with me?

Oblivious to my thoughts Lily sipped her tea. "This food is very good."

"I got it from the Jade Palace. Have you ever been there?"

Lily picked up her fork. "No, but I heard it's quite nice. The building looks impressive enough."

I paused. "Would you like to go there sometime?"

"Yes, I would."

We ate in silence for a minute. "Lily there's something I learned about my aunt. It's personal but I want to share it with you."

Lily looked at me with a concerned expression. "Are you sure?"

"I want to talk to someone about it and I trust you." I put down my fork. "When I was cleaning out the basement this summer I found several bundles of letters in an old suitcase. After I read one or two I realized they were from someone she was very close to, perhaps having a romantic relationship with." This sounded so Victorian but I went on.

"The letters were postmarked Iron Mountain,

Michigan. They stopped in 1970. I could tell from the stationery and handwriting they were from a woman."

Lily looked at me intently but remained silent.

"From some pictures taken on a trip to Europe with my aunt I managed to identify the woman as Laura Gorman." I told her in detail about my efforts to locate her.

"They never found out where Laura went or what happened to her. June Gorman and her husband wondered if she had met some man and taken off with him. I just don't think so. Not from the letters." I added, "As soon as I realized what the letters were I didn't read any more. I felt it would have been intruding."

"But you cared enough to try to find out what happened to your aunt's friend."

Lily was leaning forward and for a moment I thought she would take my hand as she extended hers on the table. I looked at her pale hand with the long delicate fingers and could easily imagine her playing the piano I would eventually buy.

I finished my tea. "Thank you for listening to this story. Let's open some wine and go into the living room."

Lily sat on the couch opposite the fireplace. I went to an armchair to the side of the fireplace.

"Julie, sit over here." Lily patted the end of the couch.

I moved over and sat down. I was acutely aware of Lily sitting a few feet from me and tried to think of something to keep the conversation going. Earlier I had noticed she was wearing an interesting necklace, a leaping gold dolphin with a diamond eye.

"I like your necklace."

"Thank you." Lily fingered it. "This was a present."

I waited uneasily to hear from whom she had received it.

"A year ago I was Christmas shopping in the mall and saw this in a jewelry store. I thought about it all week and then went back and bought it for myself. My Christmas present."

"I like that."

Lily indicated the presents under the tree. "Would you like to open your present?"

"Oh, yes." I retrieved both presents from under the tree, handed her the present from me and sat down to open mine.

As I carefully tore off the wrapping I saw a large book on Queen Anne houses. Eagerly I paged through it. There were beautiful color photos of homes, original plans, drawings and a history.

"I love this book, look there's a house like mine." I held the book out for Lily to see, then went back to turning the pages. When I looked up Lily was gazing at me with an expression I couldn't label. Maybe tender was the best way to describe it.

Lily quickly looked down at the package in her lap. "I'm glad you like it. Let me open mine." She removed the Christmas paper. "Julie, how did you know I wanted this?" She held up the CD and turned it over.

"Once you told me you heard part of it on WPR."

"I can't wait to play it. Thank you so much."

"Would you like some more wine?"

Lily looked up from her CD. "Yes, please."

When I came back with our glasses Lily was standing at the window with the curtain pulled back.

"Look Julie, it's snowing."

I went over and stood behind her. I could smell the scent of her hair and see the delicate curve of her throat. Outside, large snowflakes were gently floating down.

"I don't think it will amount to anything but it's beautiful." She continued to watch the snow falling.

When she dropped the curtain and turned around I reluctantly stepped back.

"This is perfect for Christmas Eve." I turned the lights down and opened the curtains so we could watch the snow.

Lily stretched and sipped her wine. "This is so enjoyable. The lovely tree, fire in the fireplace, your magnificent house." She looked at me with a half smile. "And the company."

My heart jumped. What did she mean?

"I imagine you'll have a good time at the party tomorrow." More exciting than tonight, I thought.

"It's an open house. This is what I enjoy." She picked up her glass. "I believe you said you were going to Milwaukee for New Year's."

"My friends wanted me to come for Christmas but I wanted to be here. I said I'd come for New Year's." I really wasn't looking forward to a big New Year's celebration.

"Do you miss Milwaukee and your friends? Do you think you might eventually move back there?"

"We really only worked together." I hesitated. "And had a few other things in common. This is my home now. No, I'm not going back."

Lily was looking at the tree. "Did you come here for Christmas as a child?"

"Only once. The Christmas after my father died. I was small and the tree looked enormous although it was probably the size of this one." I paused and then decided to tell the rest.

"My father was my Aunt Margaret's younger brother, there were just the two of them, and I don't think she and my mother got along. There wasn't any outright trouble but I could always sense their dislike of each other. After my mother died I came here for Christmas when I was at the university but then my aunt only had a small tabletop tree."

I knew Lily had a brother who lived in Seattle and since she didn't mention her parents I assumed they had died. She didn't offer anything about them and I didn't ask.

In the past, Christmas had never been a special time for me. Shopping, eating, parties at work, bad arrangements of Christmas favorites blaring everywhere and garish decorations.

Tonight was different. It wasn't just the house or the tree. It was Lily's presence. I shifted on the couch so I could look at her. In her low, gentle voice she was relating an anecdote about an orchestra she had played with in another town several years ago.

"Since it was a municipal orchestra, it was open to anyone who wanted to join. One semester we started with the usual violins, but only one cello, one horn and twelve flutes. It was quite a challenge for the conductor to find music for us to play." She laughed.

Even Lily's laugh was special for me. I added, "The flute is a pretty popular instrument. Easy to carry."

"Eventually, six of the flutes fell by the wayside and we acquired another cello. I love the fact that our orchestra is so well balanced."

I tried to think of something interesting to say, but gave up. With Lily I didn't feel I had to be entertaining her every minute. We sat in a comfortable silence sipping our wine and watching the snow fall, although I was acutely aware of her thigh inches from mine.

"Vickie said we would be playing the Kalinnikov Symphony No. 1 but I don't think I've ever heard it."

"I have the CD. I'll give it to you to take home. I've listened to it a couple of times. Lovely."

We finished the wine. Lily ran her hand through her hair and looked at her watch. "Midnight already, I didn't realize it was so late, I really better go." She paused. "This has been such a nice evening for me."

I wished there were a raging blizzard out there and she would be forced to stay overnight. Instead, it remained a gentle, picturesque snowfall with little accumulation. I got her coat and scarf and then we stood close together in the front hall as she put them on.

"Thank you for the thoughtful present and sharing your home with me."

Before I could reply she put her hand on my shoulder, leaned over and kissed my cheek. I opened the door; she turned and walked down the steps to her car in the driveway. I stood there in a state of shock from the kiss, the warmth of her lips, as I waved to her and watched her car drive up the street.

Inside, I turned off the tree lights and blew out the candles. The kiss hadn't been passionate or sexual, just a simple, quick kiss. I told myself it wasn't terribly unusual for women to embrace each other or give a peck on the cheek.

In my bedroom I opened the curtains so I could watch the snowflakes in the light of the streetlamp. It had been such a perfect evening that as I lay in bed and finally closed my eyes I hoped the bad dreams about the fire wouldn't return to haunt me.

CHAPTER FOURTEEN

"Gertrude, get down!" Ginger leaned over and grabbed the dog's collar pulling her back in time to avert my jeans being clawed to pieces.

I moved sideways through the doorway into their apartment clutching my suitcase and the large bag holding their presents.

Cindy stepped up to me. "Here, let me help you. Gertrude is so hyper with all the people coming and going for the holiday season."

I took my things into the spare bedroom and then joined my friends in the living room. Cindy brought a plate of cheese and crackers and although it was five o'clock with a long night ahead of us, Ginger was already drinking a beer. I saw she was wearing a new Packers sweatshirt. I had brought along three bottles of wine and Ginger opened one, poured me a glass and went over to the stereo. Mannheim Steamroller blasted from the speakers. Ginger waved her hands in rhythm to "Deck The Halls."

"This is an old recording but I love it. I get it out every Christmas."

Cindy shouted, "It's giving me a headache. Turn it down."

Laughing, Ginger moved over to the stereo and lowered the volume.

I sank down on the couch with my glass and looked around the apartment. An unnaturally bright green artificial tree stood in the corner, the kind where the branches always reminded me of toilet brushes. The tree decorations consisted of dogs resembling Gertrude, deer, snowmen and an assortment of Packers ornaments.

Seeing me looking at the tree Ginger gestured toward it. "You remember, we can't have a real tree. Some fire regulations I guess."

On the end table next to me an ornate nativity set rested on a layer of cotton wool giving the impression there had been a heavy snowfall in Bethlehem. A sprig of artificial mistletoe dangled from the doorway between the kitchen and living room. I took a sip of my wine and looked over at Cindy. She looked cute in an expensive red wool sweater with white reindeer prancing across the chest. "I like your sweater."

"Thanks, a Christmas present from Ginger. You look cool."

I was wearing my favorite outfit, a black wool turtleneck sweater and jeans.

"Here's the plan, Julie. We're going to This Is The Place first and then to Marge's. She's having an open house." Seeing my expression Ginger continued. "I know what you're thinking but if you get her away from work she's okay."

Cindy added, "Yes, she really has a heart of gold."

At the lab Marge was what I'd thought of as a high-maintenance employee. Over the years our supervisor had her hands full with her, trying everything including sending her to the Employee Assistance Program for counseling, to no avail. When Marge came to work in the morning she set the tone for the day. If she was in a bad mood everyone was tense and anxious. If she was in a good mood, joking and laughing, there was universal relief. I had gotten along with her as best I could. I disliked confrontation and stayed away from her as much as possible when she was in one of her stormy moods.

At about eight we piled into Cindy's Mustang and drove to This Is The Place, the latest "in" bar which would probably last another year before being replaced by another more popular place and then go out of business.

On the way I thought about what Lily would be doing tonight. She had called me on Christmas Day before she left for the open house to thank me for the evening at my house. I asked if she had plans for New Year's Eve.

"Yes, some of the faculty and staff go out for dinner together. This year we're going to Tosca. Vickie's in charge of the arrangements. It's Italian and supposed to be excellent."

"Have a good time and Happy New Year." I was going to mention I had been there with Vickie but Lily continued to speak and the moment passed.

"Be sure to have a safe trip and Happy New Year, Julie."

When we entered This Is The Place, New Year's hats and horns were being handed out. A small artificial tree draped in Packers green and gold stood on the back bar and red and green Christmas streamers hung from the ceiling. Tonight, large numerals covered with sparkle and spelling out "1999" were tacked to the wall.

We pushed our way through the crowd to the bar. I ordered a light beer. This wasn't a place for wine drinkers—Cindy once described their chardonnay as cat piss. The air was filled with smoke, it seemed everyone here tonight was a smoker.

Ginger waved to someone across the room. "There's Nicole." She leaned down to me to be heard over the jukebox and the screaming and laughter. "She heard we were bringing an unattached friend but lost interest when she heard you live in Green River." Ginger laughed. "I guess she doesn't want a long-distance romance."

I looked over at the woman who had waved to Ginger. She had short dark hair and a slim body and was holding court with three other women as she sipped her beer and smoked her cigarette.

I stood clutching my beer glass, mostly as a prop, taking an occasional sip. The place was jammed and I was jostled as groups of women crowded past me and the occasional unsteady drinker fell against me. I imagined Lily having an elegant meal tonight with her faculty and staff friends. I wondered what she was wearing and who she was talking to, and I could picture Vickie as the center of attention at the party.

Ginger came back from talking to someone she knew at the other end of the room, took my arm to get my attention and leaned down so I could hear her.

"Enough of this place, we're going to Marge's, Nicole is coming along too."

Twenty minutes later Ginger, Cindy and I climbed the front steps of Marge's duplex and rang the doorbell. The door flew open.

"Happy New Year, come on in!" Marge was in her slightly hysterical, happy mood. As we filed in, I clutching the two bottles of wine I brought as my contribution to the evening, Marge saw me and shrieked, "Julie, how great to see you!"

I was grabbed and embraced by Marge. I awkwardly returned the embrace and then gently disentangled myself. I had not been brought up in a family that hugged. The very idea of my aunt or mother hugging someone was faintly humorous.

"I've missed you, I don't know why you left the lab, and oh you brought wine, how nice. Let's see. Maybe put it in the kitchen, forget the refrigerator, we'll probably open it right away."

Marge, who was in her late forties, had her short brown hair newly done in a rigid style and was wearing brown wool slacks and a short tan Ultrasuede jacket over a crisp white blouse. It was a nice change from her shapeless lab coat.

"Dad's upstairs, I gave him lots of snacks, his favorite television show is on and don't worry about noise. He's kind of hard of hearing."

I remembered that Marge and her father shared the duplex.

Nicole arrived next and then Beth and her husband. "We can't stay long," Beth said, "we're on our way to another party."

Ginger and Cindy stared sourly at Beth and Ginger mumbled, "Then why bother coming at all?" I could see their relationship hadn't changed.

Beth looked around the room, spied me and came over. "Julie, I heard you might be here. Can we talk?" She motioned toward a large plaid couch. We sat down, and I balanced my wineglass on my knee.

"Have you been able to find out anything about Amy's life up in that godforsaken place?"

I hesitated, trying to think what to say. I wasn't sure that anything I had learned would be helpful.

"When she moved up there she lived with a woman named Mary. They didn't get along and she moved out."

"Oh her." Beth made a dismissive gesture with her hand. "Amy needed a place to stay, you know, someone to share the rent. I don't think they had much in common."

"I heard she dated the assistant conductor of the orchestra for a while."

Beth sat up. "Really? What was she like?"

"No, a man. His name is Alan."

"A man? But I thought Amy…"

"Not unusual, Beth, and anyway it didn't last long. You know, dating could mean going out for a beer and pizza." I didn't mention that Amy had probably used Alan to get the first chair. I was uncomfortable with this conversation and hoped Beth would decide it was time for her and her husband to leave.

Beth tipped up her wineglass and drained the contents. "I'm not happy with the way the police handled Amy's disappearance. This spring I'm going up to Green River and demand they reopen the case. I'll call you when I come, Julie."

She stood up and looked down at me. "How are you doing up there? You look good." She seemed disappointed.

"Fine. I like it there."

She patted my arm and crossed the room to join her husband, a tall beefy man with a trim beard.

I went to the kitchen, poured more wine and looked forward to relaxing and observing the others at the party. That was not to be.

"Having fun? I understand you worked with all these people before the fire."

"Hi Nicole. Yes, I did."

Nicole looked around. "I'm going outside for a cigarette. Want to join me? Grab your jacket, bring your drink."

We went out to the front porch where two aluminum

chairs stood waiting for better weather. We sat on them in the light of the porch lamp, and Nicole removed a pack of cigarettes from her pocket, lit one with a disposable lighter and turned her head to blow the smoke away.

"Ginger said you moved up north somewhere but when I saw Beth I realized it was that town where her sister Amy disappeared."

I wasn't sure what to say and Nicole went on. "Did you know Amy?"

"Not very well, we just played in an orchestra together here in Milwaukee."

Nicole drew deeply on her cigarette and blew the smoke away from me. "I heard Beth talking about having the case reopened but everyone thinks Amy just took off with someone. No foul play."

"I don't know what happened to her."

Nicole continued. "Amy was down here in the bars one weekend bragging about having an affair with a professor at a college up there."

I was startled. "A professor? Are you sure?"

Nicole was defensive. "I only know what I heard her say. Besides Amy might have made it up to get attention. I wouldn't put it past her."

"I'm sure that's what Amy said. I just am so surprised." Who could it be, assuming it was true? There were so many professors at Northbrook and since Amy never had any classes there, it might have been someone she met in a bar. I could think of a couple in my department who might qualify. I dismissed the story. As Nicole said, Amy probably made it up.

Nicole puffed on her cigarette and turned to me. "If I came up to Green River what would I do? Do you have any women's bars?"

"There is one."

"I'll bet you're there all the time."

"No, I've only been there once."

"Do you have anyone special up there?"

"No." If she had asked if there was someone I wanted, the answer would have been yes.

Nicole flipped her cigarette out onto the lawn and stood up. "Let's go in, it's kind of cold out here."

Back inside and thoroughly chilled I looked for a place to warm up. A gas fireplace in the living room was blazing away so I carried my wineglass over to it and sat down on the floor. As I was warming up and starting to relax Cindy came over and sat down next to me. She motioned toward the corner of the living room where an aluminum Christmas tree stood with a spotlight shining on a revolving colored disc. A few blue ornaments hung on the tree.

"How about that tree? Marge's father had it in the attic for years."

I looked over at the tree. "Pretty neat." I thought it was impressively retro but lacking any holiday warmth.

Cindy turned her gaze away from the tree to me. "I saw Beth talking to you. Did she tell you about the lawsuit?"

"No. What lawsuit?"

Cindy sipped her beer and pushed back her dark hair. She had always been thin but looked as if she had lost some weight.

"The families of our two co-workers who died in the fire are suing the lab. We all support them, but on the other hand we're afraid the place may go out of business if the lab loses."

She took another drink. "They deserve to lose. Ginger and I are trying to find jobs somewhere else. It's a hassle driving across town to the new location and nothing is any better. Even though all the equipment was lost in the fire they bought a lot of used instruments for the new place. I'm glad for you that you left."

We sat in silence for a few minutes, then Cindy's mood seemed to lift. "Say, I think Nicole is interested in you."

This was an awkward moment. "Cindy, she really is nice but I'm not interested. It's not the right time for me."

Cindy nodded. "I understand Julie, I won't encourage her."

"Thanks Cindy."

Cindy cleared her throat nervously. "Julie, Ginger and I are worried about you living up there alone. It seems such a waste. I don't know if you know it but you're an attractive woman. In the bar tonight I saw several women looking at you. I know you inherited that house but you could sell it and move back here."

"I appreciate your concern but I really am content. I love my classes and playing in the orchestra and I've met some interesting people." A woman I wanted but couldn't get involved with and a woman who had made an advance but was too much for me.

Cindy got up from the floor. "Just remember, if you need anything we're here for you."

As I watched her cross the room to join a group who were arguing loudly over whether the 49ers or Packers would win the playoff, I reflected that Ginger and Cindy had been my good friends but I could no longer enjoy or relate to the lifestyle they and their friends led. I felt a fleeting sadness when I realized that my life was now in Green River and they would no longer be a part of it.

Just before midnight someone turned on the television and the countdown to the New Year began. At midnight there was cheering, exchanging of kisses, waving of glasses and Nicole and Ginger blew the horns they had brought from the bar.

I joined in trying to whip up some enthusiasm for the celebration. A new year. What would it bring for me? I had no idea.

CHAPTER FIFTEEN

The spring semester had begun but the weather was not spring like. Tonight was the first orchestra rehearsal of the semester and as I sat in my kitchen eating a small bowl of vegetable soup I looked out the window with increasing anxiety. It had started snowing in the early morning and showed no signs of letting up. The weather forecasts were ominous. Some predicted eight inches and others predicted twelve. I wondered if the rehearsal would be canceled. My understanding was that a telephone system was set up where we would be notified. My answering machine had been on all afternoon but there were no messages.

Thirty minutes before the rehearsal I packed up and left the house. My Jeep in the driveway was now covered with snow, requiring extensive work with the snowbrush.

When I arrived at the Fine Arts Building I entered along with the tall clarinet player. We stomped the snow from our feet and as she shook the snow from her hair she complained. "I'm really surprised Vickie didn't cancel this rehearsal, it's brutal out there. This isn't like her."

When I climbed to the stage in Stofer Hall Terri was already there standing in front of her chair arranging her damp ski jacket over the back. She told me why the rehearsal hadn't been canceled.

"Vickie's not here tonight and Alan is leading the rehearsal." She leaned closer to me. "They didn't announce she wouldn't be here. The last time we knew she wasn't going to be here hardly anyone showed up and Alan was pretty upset. I guess now it's a secret when she isn't coming."

She opened her horn case. "Katy called me that she's not coming tonight. She lives outside town and didn't want to drive in this. I don't blame her."

Karen arrived next, brushing snow from her jacket. "This is ridiculous. I wouldn't have come but it's the first rehearsal of the semester and we'll be getting the new music."

As she spoke the librarian, one of the second violin players, was busily moving between the sections distributing music.

Terri looked over at Karen. "No Vickie tonight. Alan is running the rehearsal."

"That explains it, his night to show off." Karen accepted the horn parts from the librarian and passed them down.

I took my parts and handed Terri the rest of the music. "I'll take Katy's parts, she's not coming tonight."

Karen looked at Alan with disgust. "I don't know how he got this job."

Terri leaned over and blew air into her horn to warm it up, then straightened. "I heard he had a rich, old uncle who donated a lot of money when they updated Stofer Hall. I think the community orchestra board kind of pressured Vickie into taking him on as her assistant. I mean, he's not even on the music faculty, does some kind of computer work in the admissions department."

I thought how lucky I was to sit next to Terri; she was an endless source of information.

A few minutes later I looked up to see Lily come in and join her section. Since New Year's we had only talked once on the telephone when she called to make sure I had returned safely from my trip to Milwaukee. She saw me, waved, and I started to go over to her but just then Alan rapped loudly on his stand for everyone's attention.

"How nice to see you all on this pleasant winter evening." Alan beamed, waiting for the laughter that was not forthcoming. There were instead some muttered comments about how stupid to make us come out in this weather. Embarrassed, he turned his attention to arranging the music on his stand and then looked up.

"Professor Read is out of state attending a conference. The music for the Kalinnokov will be here next week, so let's start with Beethoven's 'Egmont Overture.' After we tune."

This was a piece I had played before on at least two occasions. I really enjoyed it and hoped Alan wouldn't do anything to change that.

Tuning was an extended procedure with Alan while he listened critically, cocking his head and asking for minute adjustments from players who sounded okay to us.

We began the Egmont and my worst fears were realized. Alan started, stopped, and asked for endless tempo and dynamic adjustments. I no longer recognized the piece I loved.

Forty minutes into the rehearsal a man with short brown hair sprinkled with gray walked into the hall and up onto the stage to draw Alan's attention. He was neatly dressed in corduroy slacks and a crewneck sweater over a plaid shirt, contrasting with Alan's faded sweatshirt and jeans. Annoyed by the interruption Alan stopped our rehearsal and listened to the man who was urgently talking to him. Alan appeared to disagree with him but finally and sullenly nodded in agreement.

We all sat waiting for Alan's announcement, but the man who I vaguely remembered seeing around campus, spoke up.

"Good evening everyone. I'm David Hansen, Assistant to the President. The sheriff's department has informed us that a snow emergency has been declared. The college has made the decision to end all evening classes and cancel classes tomorrow. We would like you to end your rehearsal now so you can all get home safely."

There were comments of "about time" and "good idea" as orchestra members immediately began packing up their instruments. Terri and Karen stood up and put away their horns.

"What an idiot, making us come out in this." Karen zipped up her ski jacket and stalked off.

I looked over to the flutes where Lily was talking with her section. As I approached I heard the second flute, an older woman with curly white hair, talking to Lily. "I just called Bill to come pick me up, and we can give you a ride home. Leave your car here tonight."

They turned toward me as I joined them. The second flute explained. "Lily's car is not good in this weather, rear-wheel drive, so Bill is picking me up and we'll take her home."

I couldn't let this happen. "I can give you a ride, it's on

my way." Lily looked grateful and so did the other flute player.

Lily turned to me. "Are you sure this is all right, Julie?"

"Of course. Tomorrow after they plow I'll bring you back here to pick up your car."

When we stepped outside our feet sank into the heavy snow. In the parking lot orchestra members were brushing the snow from their cars as the engines ran to clear windshields and rear windows while the snow swirled around them.

"Do you want to get anything from your car?"

"Yes, my briefcase. I haven't been home. I had work to finish in my office, and then came right over to the rehearsal. I was shocked to see so much snow and didn't know Vickie wouldn't be here."

"I imagine she would have canceled the rehearsal."

"Yes, she would have." The falling snow glistened on Lily's hair and flakes clung to her dark lashes. She reached up and tightened her scarf to keep the snow from her throat.

Lily got her briefcase from the trunk of her car and we made our way to my Jeep. I started it and then reached behind the seat for my snowbrush. By the time I had cleared the windows and headlights my hair and jacket were covered with snow. I got in and Lily reached over to brush the snow off my hair. I felt the warmth of her bare fingers brush my cheek.

I slowly drove onto the main road leading into town. Ahead I saw flashing red and blue lights. A police car had pulled up to two cars which had collided and were off the road in the ditch. I drove carefully around them. The wind was howling and blowing the snow so hard that even with my wipers on high I was having trouble seeing ahead. My Jeep had good traction in the heavy snow but like other vehicles it wasn't any better stopping on the slick road. A

car tore past me on the right, snow flying from the rear
tires as it fishtailed.

"Look at the idiot." Lily shook her head.

Two blocks later the car had spun around and was in
the other lane facing the wrong way and in the ditch.

"At the next stoplight turn right." Lily shifted in her
seat to look at me. "Julie, why don't you stay at my place
tonight?"

Stay with Lily? How could I spend the night with her?
Would we sleep together? Could I trust myself to be with
her?

"Thanks, but I'm fine."

"I'm really worried for you, Julie. I have underground
parking so your Jeep will be out of the weather and safe."
She added, "And we don't have classes tomorrow."

By now I was increasingly nervous about driving in
what had become a raging blizzard and worried about
getting us safely home. How good it would be to stay with
her if for no other reason than to get out of this weather.

Just then an emergency vehicle, siren screaming and
lights flashing, came up behind us. I pulled over for it to
pass.

"Julie, will you stay with me?"

"Maybe I will."

After we had parked in her underground garage we
carried our cases to the stairs and up to Lily's floor. We
entered her apartment, I took off my boots and she hung
our coats in the closet.

"Come in, I'll turn up the heat."

I looked around the large living room. It was tastefully
decorated with a tan leather chair and couch, simple brass
lamps and an interesting abstract painting on the wall
depicting a flute, piano keyboard and music.

"This is very nice." Despite all the leather and brass the
room was not masculine.

Lily was occupied adjusting the thermostat. "My lease

is up the end of July so I have to make a decision. When I came here I planned to buy a house but the time has flown by. I've been so busy at the college it was more convenient to just stay here."

She turned around. "Are you hungry, Julie?"

I was but didn't want to admit it. I shrugged, "A little."

"How about a toasted cheese sandwich and whatever else I can find?"

"I'd like that."

"What should we have to drink?" She paused. "On a cold snowy evening how would hot chocolate be?" She was standing in the doorway to the small kitchen, her hair still damp from the snowflakes, and she had removed her sweater leaving the turtleneck jersey outlining her body. I couldn't take my eyes from her but she turned away.

"Hot chocolate would be great." I sat on the couch and looked at the end table piled with books and magazines.

"If I'd known I was having company I would have tidied up. Help yourself to something to read," she called from the kitchen.

We ate in the small dining area and Lily looked at me as she sipped her hot chocolate. "I'm already looking forward to spring and our winter has only just begun."

"I agree. When I see my first robin I'll be so happy."

"Your first robin of spring. Do you know what Emily Dickinson wrote?" She recited: "I dreaded that first robin so."

"She did? Why?"

"One interpretation is that she finds the recurrence of spring threatening. It's physical evidence that time is moving forward and a future she dreads continues to approach."

"How sad."

"Yes." Lily set down her cup and pushed back her dark hair. "Are you having a garden this summer?"

"I'm going to have a plot with some vegetables. I'll have heirloom tomatoes and some other stuff."

"Vickie has a big garden behind her house but it's overgrown and crammed with plants. Not what I like as a garden and there is an oddly shaped fishpond."

"One of those forms you buy?"

Lily shook her head. "No, it was concrete or cement. Most fishponds I've seen are round or square, this was long and narrow like a miniature lap pool. I think she did it herself and there was a tree hanging over it so it was full of leaves. I would have picked a different site. Last fall I was at her house to pick up some flute parts and she had a phone call so I went out to walk in the garden. When she came out she was angry I was there. Most people are so proud of their gardens. I guess Vickie is a little eccentric— or maybe was embarrassed by how hers looked."

She laughed and I was only aware of her warmth and closeness. Who cared about Vickie's fishpond? "Yes, they always want to show them off or better still get them on a garden tour."

"Julie, I put towels and a new toothbrush for you in the bathroom. I have a spare bedroom I use as an office. I put a pair of pajamas on the futon."

She looked out the window at the swirling snow. "I got the futon thinking my brother would like to stay here with me during a business trip. But he stayed at a hotel in Green Bay. His company paid for it." She looked back and smiled. "So, you will be the first person to sleep on it."

I could tell she had been hurt by her brother's behavior. "I'm honored."

We were both suppressing yawns. Lily had put in a long day at the college and I was finally relaxing after the tense drive from the college.

I changed into Lily's pajamas, brushed my teeth and lay down pulling the covers over me.

The next thing I heard was, "Julie, are you all right?"

Lily was sitting on my bed next to me with her hand on my shoulder.

I sat up abruptly and looked at Lily.

"You were talking about a fire and calling for help."

I fell back on the pillow. "There was a bad fire. At the lab where I worked. Two of our co-workers were trapped inside. They died."

"How awful, Julie" Lily removed her hand from my shoulder and carefully pushed a strand of hair away from my face. Her voice was gentle and her face soft with concern. "Do you feel guilty because you survived and they didn't?"

"I don't know. Maybe I do."

"Was there anything you could have done?"

"Oh no, we didn't know they were still in there."

"How do your other co-workers feel?"

I thought for a moment. "I guess they feel lucky they escaped."

"Do they still talk about it and are they upset?"

I didn't remember that the fire had been discussed when I was with them in Milwaukee recently. Only speculation about the lawsuit against the company and complaints about the new lab's location.

"I don't know how they feel." I should have asked, I realized.

Lily lifted up the covers. "Move over, I'll stay with you until you fall asleep."

I started to protest, then stopped. I turned on my side to make enough room in the narrow bed for Lily who lay down and pulled the covers over us. She slipped her arm around my waist and I took her hand and held it. I could feel the warmth of her body against mine. How would I be able to sleep?

The next I knew, sunlight was pouring in around the blinds. I sat up and Lily appeared in the doorway, fully dressed.

"Good morning." She looked relaxed and fresh. "The snow stopped a few hours ago and the plows have been out. I was just getting the coffee ready."

I sat up on the edge of the bed. I was probably a mess, my hair rumpled, and I still felt groggy. "Coffee sounds great."

We ate breakfast together, scrambled eggs and toast, and then I drove Lily back to the college to pick up her car. This trip was so different from last night. The sun was shining, the roads were plowed and the traffic moved as usual.

In the Fine Arts Building parking lot I used my snowbrush on Lily's car while she started it and got the defroster going. Her car was soon cleared of snow and I stood at the driver's side as she lowered the window.

"I can't thank you enough for driving me home last night." She put her hand up to shield her eyes from the sun.

I looked at Lily and wished we were just starting for her apartment and reliving last night. This morning she looked so youthful. Her hair was pulled back and fastened with a barrette, her jacket was unzipped and the flannel shirt under it was open at the neck.

"Thank you for letting me stay with you." I smiled. "I liked your futon."

Lily started to say, "Maybe we..." and then stopped. I stood with my hand on the windowsill. Our faces were inches apart. If I leaned in we would be touching.

"Thanks again, Julie." Lily hesitated and then rolled up her window.

I watched her drive out of the parking lot as we waved to each other. I wanted to run after her and ask her to take me home with her again. This time if I was in bed with her I wouldn't just fall asleep. But would she have wanted more? Why did I have so much trouble showing my emotions? Perhaps because I was brought up being told it was wrong.

When I returned to my house I found Dorothy's snow removal service had also cleared my sidewalk, leaving only the driveway for me to shovel. As I began clearing the driveway I was glad to have something physical to do to take my mind off the thoughts of last night that swirled through my head.

As I worked I could not ignore what Lily had spoken of about my possible guilt feelings after the fire in the lab. Perhaps she was right. There was nothing I could have done to affect the outcome and none of my former co-workers seemed to have suffered emotionally as I had.

As I looked up at the cupola on the garage with a weather vane of ducks frozen in flight and the bright sun shining down on the fresh snow, I thought of a line from the Handel oratorio *Samson*. "To fleeting pleasures make your court, no moment lose, for life is short." I decided it was time to put the accident at the lab behind me and move on with my life. Once I had had dreams and hopes for the future. It was time to reclaim them.

CHAPTER SIXTEEN

Lily threw back the covers and sat up on the edge of the bed. Four thirty in the morning and she had been lying awake for over an hour. Putting on her slippers she went into the bathroom and drank a glass of water. Then she went into the living room and pulled back the curtain.

With only the faint illumination of a streetlamp, the street was dark and deserted at this hour. She let the curtain drop and returned to her bed, pulling the down comforter up to her chin, brushing her breasts and triggering memories of making love with Vickie.

What was wrong? She never had trouble sleeping.

She knew what was wrong. Her carefully arranged life had been disrupted since the day she'd seen the woman in the Continuing Education Office. At first it was enjoyable and interesting to meet her over a drink together after rehearsal. Christmas Eve together had been a comfortable and pleasurable time. It had been touching how Julie tried to please her and show her the house she obviously loved. But why had she asked Julie to stay with her the night of the snowstorm? Julie probably could have made it home safely in her Jeep. And why had she gotten in bed with her? She told herself it was because she felt sorry for her when she learned of the horrible fire she had survived and wanted to comfort her. Face it, she thought, you really wanted to take her in your arms and make love to her. No, that wasn't true. Julie had been so distraught it wouldn't have been the right time. For all she knew, when Julie went to Milwaukee it might have been to see another woman, or a man. Was it because she was older that she was hesitant to be the one to initiate a relationship with Julie?

With Vickie it had been different. Almost immediately Vickie had declared her intentions and Lily had been eager. Before Vickie, Lily had had a brief affair in graduate school, which ended when the woman decided that she preferred men. At her last college in Minnesota there had been Janet, the tennis coach. Their affair lasted barely a year when Janet chose a job offer in Texas over Lily.

Now, there was a new complication. Lately Vickie had been making advances, signaling that she wanted to resume their relationship. As attractive as Vickie was, that was not going to happen. The desire, affection and passion she had once felt for Vickie was gone forever. The hurt of her betrayal still remained.

As she lay there she resolved to get her life back to the comfortable routine she had been following before she met Julie.

Finally she fell asleep.

CHAPTER SEVENTEEN

One o'clock in the afternoon and the intense winter sunlight poured through the windows of the Union cafeteria onto my table. Classes had resumed following the snowstorm and today the temperature had dropped. I finished my coffee and turkey sandwich, and as I made my way through the crowd I saw Lily looking at the long line.

"Lily, how are you?"

She looked startled. "Hello Julie. I was going to get a cup of coffee to take back to my office but I don't have time to stand in this line."

"Bad time of the day." I smiled but she ignored me,

seeming preoccupied. "Wait, why don't I get it and bring it to your office? I'm done for the day and don't have anything else to do."

"No, I don't need it." Lily turned away.

"Do you use cream or sugar? And where's your office?"

Lily hesitated. "Black and my office is in Johnston Hall, second floor, room two hundred at the end of the hall. Thanks, Julie."

I took a place in line wondering if something had happened to upset her. Maybe it was a problem student or a demanding administrator.

Johnston Hall, one of the original older red brick buildings on the Northbrook College campus, was covered with ivy and constructed in the College Gothic design.

I climbed the worn wooden stairs to its second floor, carefully carrying my cardboard cup of coffee. When I got to Room 200 the door was partially ajar. I knocked and entered.

Lily looked up but without the usual smile for me. I carefully set the cup on her desk away from the papers and her computer.

"Thank you." She reached for it, seeming preoccupied.

I backed away. "See you at rehearsal next week."

As I got to the door she called, "Julie, thank you."

When I got home I was still confused over her behavior. Somehow I had to do something to put it out of my mind. In the park, the cross-country ski trails wove through the woods while the golf course was the place to snowshoe. There I could be alone. Even on a weekday, retirees or people on their day off used the ski trail.

I tramped around the golf course for over an hour until I was exhausted and the sun was starting to set.

At home, when I had thawed out, I took a hot shower, heated a can of turkey chili and debated whether to have a glass of wine or cup of tea with it. The tea won out as I opened the wooden tea chest filled with a variety of teas, which had been a Christmas present from Ginger and Cindy.

"We thought up in the north woods you must drink a lot of tea and coffee." Green River wasn't exactly the north woods, but it was a thoughtful gift.

I had just put on a CD of the Brahms *Fourth Symphony* and settled down with one of my textbooks when the phone rang.

"I hope I'm not disturbing you, Julie."

"No, Lily, I was just having a cup of tea." Had I done something wrong?

"I wanted to apologize for my behavior this afternoon. It was so good of you to spend all that time standing in line to bring me the coffee."

"It's all right. I still had time to go snowshoeing this afternoon."

"You did? Where?"

"At the county park near here."

"It sounds like fun."

"Just a lot of walking around, but a good excuse to be outdoors and get some exercise. Did you ever go snowshoeing?"

"No, but I think I would like it."

"The Green River Nature Center rents them. Would you like to go sometime? Maybe this Saturday?"

"I'd love to, it's a date."

A date? Was she only using an expression?

"I'll pick you up at one o'clock if that's okay. Be sure and dress warmly and wear boots."

"I will." She paused. "And thank you again."

When I hung up everything was wonderful.

***

It had snowed during the night and today, Saturday,

a light fluffy snow added to the existing cover as the sun shone brightly.

Lily came out the door of her apartment building looking stylish in a burgundy ski jacket, jeans and boots while carrying a knit cap and gloves.

"Hi Julie, I think I'm going to enjoy this." Lily climbed into the Jeep, turned to me and smiled warmly.

As excited as I was and as much as I looked forward to the day, all I could manage to say was, "Do you have your sunglasses?"

Lily patted her jacket pocket. "Right here."

At the Nature Center we walked over to the shed where snowshoes were rented and as we entered I saw Jim and Carol from my bird-watching class. Carol was bundled up in a puffy brown down-filled jacket and colorful knit stocking cap complete with a large tassel.

"Well, Julia, how are you? We haven't seen you since that bird-watching class. You didn't come back."

I cringed and mumbled, "I got so busy with moving and didn't have the time." I tried to change the subject. "My friend would like to rent snowshoes."

Jim stepped forward, no doubt anxious to help an attractive woman. "Sit right here on this bench and I'll get a pair for you." Jim wore a matching stocking cap but in a more subdued color. They were probably a knitting project of Carol's.

While he busied himself attaching the snowshoes to Lily's boots I sat on a bench and strapped mine on.

Carol peered down at them. "You have those new aluminum ones. We only have the wooden style here. In fact, we just completed snowshoe-making classes last week."

I tried to think of something to say to defend my too-modern snowshoes but Carol had moved on.

"Julia, you'll be pleased to know we're breaking ground in March for the new building here. We had a fund drive starting last summer and now we're going to be able to have a separate wing for lectures, classes and a library." She leaned closer as another couple came in the door. "It's going to be called the Margaret Burke Education Center."

She beamed as I tried to recall if I had received a request for a donation to the Center's building fund. If I did, I must have tossed it out. Luckily, Lily was ready and we stood up and plodded toward the door.

"Trails are in good shape, what with the new snow and all." Jim watched us leave as we thanked him and waved goodbye.

We put on our sunglasses and moved down a path to the snowshoe trail. I was just ahead of Lily and turned back to her.

"The only thing to remember is—" Just then Lily pitched forward onto me and we fell in a heap in the snow on the side of the path with Lily on top of me.

"Oh Julie, I'm so sorry. Are you all right?"

"Yes, no problem." I struggled to my feet, but one of my snowshoes was trapped under Lily's and I fell back down on top of her. Lily was laughing. Really laughing, something I had not seen her do since I met her. I joined in and finally I got up and gave Lily my hand, pulling her to her feet.

As we brushed the snow off each other Lily looked toward the shed. "I'm glad your friends didn't see us. What a comedy. What were you going to tell me before I fell on you?"

"Just to remember to keep your feet far enough apart that you don't step on them."

"A little late I guess. Let's go."

We started down the path onto the trail and soon Lily was moving smoothly along, her dark hair under her knit cap flying behind her. She had a natural fluid grace that I imagined would help her with any sport.

As we moved along we paused to look at a stream, now

frozen over, which ran through the Nature Center with a rustic wooden bridge arching over it while two huge willow trees next to it leaned over toward the water. The air was still except for the occasional chirping of birds.

Once a wiry older woman in a green parka came up behind us at a rapid pace and we stepped aside to let her pass. Lily looked after her. "Why rush? It's just so pleasant out here that I enjoy taking my time to look at everything."

We covered both trails and after about an hour and a half returned to the shed. Jim and Carol were engaged in a conversation about building bluebird nest boxes with the woman who had passed us on the trail. She looked vaguely familiar from the bird-watching class.

Carol nodded to us as we left and I heard her say to the woman, "That's Margaret Burke's niece."

"Which one?"

"The tall blonde."

Out in the Jeep Lily removed her hat and ran a comb through her dark hair. "Would you like to have a drink and get something to eat?"

I didn't think I had a comb with me. "Yes. Do you have a place in mind?"

"How about the brew pub that opened two weeks ago?"

"Sounds great." I started the Jeep and headed there.

Inside the Green River Brew Pub large gleaming tanks, or whatever they were called, were arranged along the front of the place behind a glass partition, and the high ceiling had that open industrial look with all the beams and ducts exposed. We picked a polished wooden table near the wall. A waitress, or server, approached our table and dropped a beer coaster in front of each of us.

"Professor de Gramont! Great to see you here."

The server, young with clear skin, a slim body and long reddish hair, was gazing with obvious admiration at Lily who looked up from her beer menu.

"Jill, nice to see you."

"Have you been here before? You know we just opened two weeks ago and we're doing pretty well."

"No, I haven't. What do you recommend?"

"I like the honey ale." Jill leaned over Lily's shoulder and pointed to a selection on the menu.

"That sounds good. Jill, this is Julie."

"Pleased to meet you, Julie." Jill turned her attention back to Lily.

Jill quickly returned with our glasses of beer, which she placed carefully in front of us. It looked as if she was going to hang around but just then a party of five came in. She looked over at them with an expression of unhappiness. "Sorry, I have to go wait on them. I'll check back with you." Jill gave Lily a last adoring look and reluctantly moved away.

It occurred to me that I wasn't the only one who found Lily attractive. Probably many of her students, men and women, felt that way.

Apparently oblivious to Jill's attention Lily sipped her beer. "What was that business about bird-watching? I didn't know you were interested."

I sighed. "When I first moved here I signed up for a bird-watching class at the Nature Center. It was kind of a disaster. When the leader asked me what my favorite bird was I said robin. Pretty ordinary for bird experts."

Lily smiled. "Julie and her robins. I think I'll join the Nature Center. Maybe we could both give it a try this summer." She picked up a food menu. "What was that about your aunt?"

"She left a lot of money to the Green River Nature Center so they're going to name part of the new building after her. Good thing they don't know she left me the rest of her money or they'd want another wing from me."

Lily laughed and laid down her menu. "I enjoyed snowshoeing today. I work out at the college exercise facility and I walk, but this was something different. You know, I would like to buy a bicycle this spring. I suppose you have one."

"Yes, and a bike rack that holds two bikes." I tentatively offered, "We could go to one of the bike paths to ride."

"Could you help me pick one out?"

"Sure, there is a good bicycle shop in the mall west of town. They can help us find something you'll like." I had to ask. "Will you be staying around this summer?"

"Oh yes. I'm teaching in summer school. What about you?"

"I'm taking some classes. I'd like to get my horticulture degree and then start graduate work."

"Good for you. Are you going to do landscape designs for rich people's homes? Oh sorry," she said impishly, "I forgot you're rich."

"No Lily." I laughed. "I want to go into plant pathology."

Lily frowned. "I'm not sure what that is. A kind of plant doctor?"

"In a way, yes. It's the study of plant diseases caused by pathogens and environmental conditions. They specialize in keeping plants healthy."

Lily grinned. "You'll have a lot of happy patients." She leaned back in her chair, tilted her head and looked at me. "Looks like we're going to have a busy summer."

I picked up my beer in confusion. Did she mean this? Joining the Nature Center, going bird-watching and biking together? I looked out the window at the snow on the ground. I couldn't wait for spring.

CHAPTER EIGHTEEN

I left my Concepts of Applied Entomology class and stopped to peer out the windows in the hallway of the Gardner Science Building.

It was a cold, overcast day and snow was predicted for later in the evening. As I stood there deciding what to buy for supper on my way home I heard someone behind me call my name.

"Hi Julie. How are your classes going?"

I turned to see Denise standing behind me. She looked happier than the last time I had seen her. The tense, preoccupied look was gone.

"Fine. How about you?"

"I just got out of Soils lab. Pretty interesting." Denise lowered her backpack to the floor. "I'm going to the Golden Lantern for a drink and pizza. Want to join me?"

"Sure."

Outside the Golden Lantern I waited in my Jeep until I saw Denise's pickup truck pull into a parking spot in front.

At this early hour, there was a small group of women who had stopped at the Golden Lantern after work. The music played softly and there wasn't much cigarette smoke yet. Denise hung her ski jacket over the back of her chair and I unwrapped my scarf, unzipped my jacket.

We ordered our beer from the same tattooed server. Denise took a swig of hers and put her bottle down. "Mary's gone for two days. A seminar for her job. Something about local government, but she gets to stay in a hotel in Green Bay tonight."

"Good for her." I poured my beer in the glass I had to ask for.

Denise moved her bottle around on the coaster. "Mary's lease is up in June and we're thinking about getting an apartment together. Something kind of nice."

I thought of Lily telling me that her lease was up in July and wondered what she would do. Renew the lease, find a new apartment or maybe buy a house?

"And I have a job interview on Friday." Denise smiled and raised her beer bottle. "It's at Northstar Perennial Farms. You've heard of them, haven't you?"

"Sure, they're pretty well known in Wisconsin."

"They have all these greenhouses where they grow their own perennials, vegetables, herbs and a few select annuals. Just what I want to do, you know, greenhouse operations. One more semester and I'll have my degree. I can take most of the classes at night."

"Good for you. Best of luck."

The server brought us another beer. "I will be so glad to quit that garden center," Denise said fervently.

I changed the subject. "You remember I asked about Amy Leland because I worked with her sister? Well, her sister is going to come up here and try to reopen the case. When I was in Milwaukee over New Year's I met this woman who said Amy had been in the bars down there bragging about having an affair with a professor up here. It would have been someone at Northbrook."

Denise frowned and picked up her bottle. "I don't know who it could be. There's one instructor in our department who's a lesbian but she has a long-term partner, and besides she wouldn't get involved with someone like Amy."

"There's the possibility that she was lying, just trying to get attention."

Denise leaned back in her chair. "I don't think anything happened to her. She just took off. We're sitting here in this cold, dreary February weather and she's probably on a beach in Florida sipping some fancy drink."

"I suppose you're right." I imagined Amy would also be wearing a bikini. Somehow, going to Florida didn't appeal to me. I wanted to be here at home, even if it meant enduring the winter weather. I was used to it and it was a part of my life in Wisconsin.

The pizza arrived and as we started eating, two women came bursting in the door, their clothes covered with snow and stomping their feet.

"It's really coming down." The dark-haired woman shook the snowflakes from her head and took a seat at the bar. Her friend brushed the snow from her jacket.

"Bad accident on Pine Street coming into town." She looked over at Denise. "Someone said it was a professor from your school."

My immediate thought was Lily.

I asked, "What kind of car was it?"

The dark-haired woman turned on her stool. "Some small sedan. Maybe a Chevy or Ford."

"They were just getting him out. I don't know how badly he was hurt." She turned back and lifted her beer.

Thank goodness it wasn't Lily.

We finished the pizza, and I saw Denise surreptitiously checking her watch. She looked embarrassed when she saw me watching her.

"Mary is going to call me tonight from Green Bay."

I looked at my own watch. "I think I better get going. I have a paper to work on."

We split the check and left, waving to each other as we got into our vehicles. I hadn't learned anything new about Amy and I was rapidly beginning to lose interest in her disappearance.

CHAPTER NINETEEN

March arrived and its variable weather made this into the month I thought of as the doldrums. Light snowfalls alternated with warm sunny days when the dirty snow melted in spots allowing patches of grass to show through. There was not enough snow cover for skiing or snowshoeing and yet it was too early for bicycling or any summer sport.

On a gloomy day when light snow was predicted I came home from my classes to a ringing phone.

"Julie. Good, you're home. We have a problem."

I groped to identify the caller. Then I realized it was

Vickie, or Professor Read as I sometimes still thought of her.

"Karen's husband called me this morning. She had emergency gall bladder surgery, not the laparoscopic kind, but the other. It seems she will be out for six or eight weeks."

As I listened to Vickie, I wondered why she was calling me.

"This leaves us without a first horn. I don't want to call someone in, so you can step up for us."

I was so comfortable with the part I was playing and thought about my past bouts with performance anxiety. "I don't know, Professor Read, uh, Vickie."

"Julie, I need you and know you can do it. Karen's husband just left the music at my house so I'll bring it over to you. You will be at home in the next hour won't you?"

"Well, yes, but I'm not sure I—"

"Give me your address."

Forty minutes later Vickie entered the front foyer. She was wearing a black wool duffel coat with bone buttons and black fur-lined boots. As she removed her black leather gloves she looked around her.

"You live here? Do you rent this house?"

"I own it. My aunt left it to me, and I moved in this summer. This is my home now."

"That's right, you told me that." She walked into the front room and looking around nodded her approval as she handed me a folder. "Interesting house. Here are the first horn parts. I know you can handle them. No one else in the section wants to play them, or is capable. This is a community orchestra so I don't want to bring in someone to play first horn. I'll move Terri and Katy up, and I know an older woman who plays in a wind band. I think she can manage the fourth part."

I took the folder. By accepting it I had committed myself.

Vickie crossed the room to the front window and pulled the curtain aside. "A nice large yard." She let the curtain drop and then turned around. I was standing closely behind her and she looked at me with a slight smile on her face, put her hands on my shoulder and kissed me on the mouth.

I was completely taken by surprise, but before I could react she stepped back.

"Are you shocked? I don't think so, I was right about you." She picked up her purse, walked to the front door and turned back.

"We have to get to know each other. Practice that part."

She laughed, and then was gone as I stood there holding the folder of music stunned by what had just happened.

***

At our next orchestral rehearsal Lily arrived just before we began. This was unusual for her as she always arrived early. Vickie ascended the podium and everyone stopped talking.

"I have some bad news." There were murmurs from the orchestra members. "Karen, our first horn, had emergency gall bladder surgery and although she is doing well it won't be possible for her to play on our concert." She paused dramatically.

"There is good news. Julie has agreed to take on the first horn part and the rest of the section will move up. I will bring in a fourth and am confident everyone will perform capably."

Heads turned to look at the horn section. Vickie picked up her baton. "Joanne has a get well card for all of you to sign at intermission."

Looking around I didn't see Alan. I leaned over to Terri. "Where's Alan tonight?"

She whispered. "That's a story. I'll tell you at intermission."

We worked on the Weber piece and a movement of the Kalinnikov. At intermission Terri waited until Katy went out to the lobby. Terri tried to pull down her heavy wool sweater whose dancing snowflake pattern strained to cover her body as she told me, "I heard Alan spent the night in jail. He was in a bar and made a pass at a woman, and then he became belligerent and they asked him to leave. Well, he took a swing at someone and they called the police. He was let go this morning. The woman didn't want to press charges. Probably afraid he would retaliate."

She looked around for Katy. "Katy went out with him once but he made her nervous, he just seemed so unstable. He was always mad at someone. She talks with him at rehearsal but really wants to get away from him."

Terri put her horn on the chair and went over to sign the card for Karen.

Lily came over to me. "Julie, I know you will do a beautiful job."

When I met Lily in September she had a light summer tan. Now, in the winter months, her skin was pale but had a healthy glow. But tonight her dark eyes looked tired and she did not have her usual brilliant smile for me.

"I've been so busy this week." She sighed. "Professor Fox, our department chairman, broke his leg in a car accident. He's home now but I've been over there meeting with him several times. Now, I have added responsibility at the college." She slowly shook her head. "I would love to stop after the rehearsal but don't think I should. I have so much work to do tonight."

"Of course, I understand. Are you the acting department chairman?" I had to ask.

Lily sighed again and looked around at the milling musicians. "Yes. What do you think of the Kalinnikov?"

"I love it, great horn parts."

"Especially tonight when you were playing." She brushed her dark hair back. "I wanted to have my hair cut this week but haven't found the time." She paused. "I know this is March but do you think it's too early to go look at bikes?"

I shook my head. "They always have a big sale the first part of April, they should have a good selection."

"Can I call you and arrange a time to go? Maybe a Saturday."

"Sure. Just let me know."

"Elisabeth, can I speak to you about a passage?"

We both turned to see Vickie standing behind us holding a rolled up piece of music, which she tapped against her leg.

"Yes, Vickie." Lily didn't appear too enthusiastic but was polite as usual.

I moved away, but looking back I could see Vickie leaning closer and asking Lily something. Her reply was to shake her head. I suspected that the piece of music Vickie held was probably just an excuse to talk to Lily. They separated, the intermission was over and Vickie went to the podium. The visiting and talking among the orchestra members stopped and everyone returned to their seat without her having to call for their attention.

After the rehearsal Lily waited to walk out to the parking lot with me. As we walked together she turned to look at me.

"I really would prefer stopping for a drink together tonight but right now with Professor Fox..."

I interrupted. "I know, we can always go another time."

We parted at my Jeep. "Goodnight Julie." She looked at me, hesitated, and then walked to her car.

As I drove home I wondered if our relationship would

always be like this. Fleeting conversations, brief times together, a drink and dinner. Never anything more.

Later that night as I lay in bed trying to fall asleep I imagined what it would be like to have Lily in bed with me. I wondered what kind of lover she would be. Aggressive and demanding or cold and unresponsive? I thought she would be none of these. She would be passionate yet gentle.

When I finally fell asleep my dreams were not of the fire at the lab but of Alan grabbing Lily at the rehearsal, dragging her out to the parking lot, forcing her into his car and speeding away as I stood watching helplessly.

CHAPTER TWENTY

"Julie, how about coming down here for St. Patrick's Day?"

Ginger was calling from Milwaukee on Thursday and St. Patrick's Day was Friday.

"I have some classes tomorrow, Ginger."

"Never mind. Come Saturday, a lot of places are celebrating then."

I wasn't that excited about a trip to Milwaukee but Lily was busy with her added duties at the college and I doubted I would see her this weekend. I thought I might as well go.

"I could come Saturday afternoon."

"Great, see you then."

So, on a cold Saturday evening we climbed into Cindy's Mustang to go to Paddy's Pub. On the way Ginger explained the plans for the evening.

"They're having live music tonight. Guaranteed to be real Irish performers. By the way, I love your sweater."

I was wearing an expensive green wool turtleneck. "Thanks, I got it on sale. Everything's spring clothes now."

We found a parking spot three blocks away and walked back to the bar. A huge white tent had been erected over the parking lot and it was now crowded with people wandering around carrying their beer or whiskey. At one end, two men stood on a low stage playing a guitar and flute. Cindy pointed to a long table set up along one side of the tent and leaned over to shout, "I want to get something to eat. I hope they have corned beef and cabbage."

I waited in line for a plastic cup of Guinness and then wandered over to listen to the flute player. His flute was wooden and only had a few keys, it looked like six, and although his playing was nimble he didn't sound anything like the silver flutes I was used to hearing. In fact, he sounded reedy, almost like a bagpipe. Certainly not like Lily's beautiful tone.

An older woman wearing a heavy cream-colored Irish sweater sat at a table next to the stage with a display of CDs for sale. I looked them over and then picked out one with a photo of the fellow with his flute. I thought maybe Lily would find it interesting. As I put my change away I looked up to see Cindy standing next to me.

"Oh, you bought a CD. Did you really like his playing?" She made a face. "He's good but it's a different sound."

"I got this for a flute player in the orchestra. I don't know what she'll think of it."

"Someone you're interested in? What's she like?"

"A professor at the college, a talented flute player, smart and a nice person."

"What does she look like?"

"Very good looking. Beautiful."

Cindy looked baffled. "Why don't you make a play for her?"

"I don't know anything about her personal life, or her sexual orientation." This sounded so prissy. "I keep thinking an old boyfriend might show up."

Cindy rolled her eyes, shook her head and changed the subject. "Say, remember Nicole from the New Year's Eve party? Well, she met someone and they moved to Florida."

"Maybe she'll run into Amy since a couple of the people I talked to think she went down there."

Cindy and I clapped as the flute player stepped off the stage followed by the guitar player. She sipped her beer. "It's hard to believe she never contacted Beth. I know she didn't get along with her mother but she could have at least sent Beth a note instead of letting her worry about her."

"From what I've learned about Amy she wasn't the most thoughtful person."

"I guess not. There's Ginger, I'm going over there."

Cindy left and a large woman in a long black wool coat climbed onto the stage carrying a guitar.

As the evening progressed it was becoming colder and colder in the tent. I had a leather jacket over my heavy sweater but I was starting to shiver and my feet were cold.

After some feedback from the speaker the woman launched into a mournful ballad. When she finished there was a sprinkling of applause and she began singing another similar song.

I wiggled my toes in my shoes and put my free hand in my jacket pocket to warm it. When I turned around Ginger was standing behind me.

"This woman is depressing and this tent is freezing. Let's get out of here."

"Fine with me."

We collected Cindy and walked up the street to the car. Ginger got behind the wheel.

"We might as well go to This Is The Place. It'll be jammed but at least warm."

This Is The Place was indeed warmer with all the bodies crowded into the smoky bar.

As "Believe" blasted out of the jukebox Ginger grimaced. "I like Cher okay but I'm already sick of that song. You'd think they'd play Irish music. I'll get us a beer." She pushed her way to the bar.

As I looked around it seemed the crowd was getting younger every time I came here. I did recognize a few old-timers who would probably always be here.

Where the tent was cold this bar was getting warmer and warmer. I unzipped my jacket.

Cindy came over to me. "See that woman standing at the end of the bar? She has a big job in public relations with the telephone company. I'm pretty sure she doesn't go with anybody." Cindy waved and I looked at a thin pretty woman with medium-length blond hair. She was talking to another couple and waved back to Cindy.

How was I supposed to meet this woman? Why would I want to? I only wanted Lily.

When Ginger suggested we leave I was relieved and ready to go. Maybe the bar scene wasn't for me anymore.

Back at their apartment none of us felt like drinking so Cindy made coffee.

As Ginger put her feet up on a footstool Gertrude the dog bounded into the room, stopped and then shook herself sending a shower of white fur into the air. I grabbed my coffee cup off the floor as she came my way.

"Next month we both have vacation time scheduled,

and we're going to Florida to check out jobs, maybe move there," Ginger said.

Cindy balanced her cup on her lap. "There're supposed to be lots of health care opportunities. With all those old people down there." Ginger and Cindy had met when they worked together in a hospital lab.

"We're so tired of the commute across town to the lab, especially this winter. We considered buying a small house near the lab but the future of the place is uncertain. You know the families of the women who died in the fire are suing the lab."

Cindy added, "The talk is that the lab had several safety violations."

I asked, "What happened to the old lab?"

"They demolished it. Too much damage and the neighbors were complaining."

I no longer had the dreams of the lab since the night I stayed with Lily. Maybe demolishing and removing it also helped in some remote way.

Ginger looked at me. "Julie, why don't you consider moving to Florida?"

"No, I don't think so."

Cindy spoke up. "She has her eye on someone in Green River."

I didn't answer and then Ginger yawned and we all went to bed. Much as I liked Gertrude I made sure my bedroom door was shut tightly so I wouldn't have her sleeping on the bed with me.

After breakfast the next morning I left for home.

On the drive home I thought about Ginger and Cindy possibly moving to Florida. I would miss them but they would invite me down there and maybe a trip to Florida during a cold winter month would be attractive.

When I arrived in Green River the weather was overcast and cold. Patches of dirty snow still remained in areas that were in the shade.

In the house I turned up the thermostat and looked around with satisfaction at my now familiar home. In what was going to be my office I saw the answering machine was flashing one message. I pressed play.

"Hi Julie, this is Lily. I've been so busy I just realized St. Patrick's Day is being celebrated this weekend. Knowing you are Irish you probably have plans. If you don't have anything planned, would you like to go someplace tonight for drinks and dinner? If I don't hear from you I'll see you Monday at orchestra rehearsal. Bye now."

The message was left Saturday at one in the afternoon. Probably just shortly after I left for Milwaukee. I stood there staring down at the phone thinking, "Oh, Lily why didn't you call just a little earlier."

CHAPTER TWENTY-ONE

On a dreary Monday evening following my trip to Milwaukee I arrived at Stofer Hall for our orchestra rehearsal. Terri was already seated and busy playing some warmup scales. After I had taken off my jacket, removed my horn from its case and arranged my music on the stand, Terri lowered her horn to her lap and leaned toward me.

"Guess what? Alan got in trouble again. He was in a fight in a bar Friday night. They tried to throw him out and he punched a guy. The police hauled him off, he's probably out of jail by now but Professor Read has had it. She's replaced him with one of her graduate students."

We both looked to the front of the room where Vickie and a thin, intense-looking young woman were talking together. Just then Lily came in and Vickie called her over and stood talking with her until it was time for the rehearsal to begin.

When Vickie stepped up on the podium the talking among the orchestra members stopped. She looked around, "I am happy to announce that Allie Freeman will be assisting me. She is one of my promising graduate students and will be conducting the 'Egmont Overture' on our upcoming concert."

Vickie stepped down and the young woman took her place to scattered applause. Allie pushed back her long brown hair and smiled pleasantly at us. She was dressed simply in black slacks and a gray turtleneck sweater and wore a minimum of makeup.

"This is a real honor for me. I have heard this orchestra play and am impressed with your talent and dedication." She looked down at the score in front of her. "Let's see if we can play the Egmont all the way through." She indicated her starting tempo and we began.

As we proceeded I was impressed and could see the other orchestra members were also. Her beat was easy to follow; she cued the different sections when necessary and was careful with the dynamic indications. We finished the rousing ending together and this time the orchestra applauded enthusiastically with Vickie smiling and joining us.

"We're going to work on the last movement of the Kalinnikov and then I'm going to dismiss the winds. Allie and I want to work with the strings for the rest of the rehearsal. But not the French horns." She looked over at us and winked.

The rest of the orchestra looked puzzled but we horns grinned knowingly. Strings operated the rotary valves on French horns. It was an old joke for horn players.

When we finished rehearsing the Kalinnikov I saw Lily waiting for me at the door.

"I left for Milwaukee just before I got your message."

"That's all right. I shouldn't have waited so late to call, I guess I was just so busy, but I'm glad you had plans."

"How is it going?" Lily looked rested and more relaxed than the last time I saw her.

"Professor Fox came back today and is going to work at least four days this week." Lily smiled. "I heard he's driving his wife crazy and she encouraged him to return to work."

"I listened to an Irish flute player Saturday night and brought you a CD of his." I removed it from my briefcase and handed it to Lily.

"Oh, thank you Julie." She examined it. "A wooden flute and it looks like only a few keys."

"You'll find it different." I had an idea. "Since we got out early would you like to come to my house? I can make us a sandwich."

"I'd love to come to your house."

We walked out to the parking lot together. "See you there." Lily waved and went to her car.

At home I got out ham, aged cheddar cheese and wheat bread. While I was cutting the cheese the knife slipped and cut my finger. I wrapped my finger in a piece of paper towel until the bleeding stopped and then hastily put on a bandage.

When Lily arrived, I hung up her jacket and she crossed the room to sit on the couch. She picked up a book lying on the table next to the couch.

"Japan, the Heian era. A fascinating time. May I look at it?"

"Yes. I'm enjoying it. Would you like wine or coffee?"

Lily looked up from paging through the book. "If it isn't too much trouble, how about a glass of wine now and coffee with our sandwiches?"

I brought the wine and stood over Lily holding her

glass. She put the book aside and looked up. "Julie! What happened to your finger?"

"I cut it trying to slice the cheese." I saw blood had seeped through the bandage.

"Let me look at it, you should change that bandage. Do you have another?" she asked anxiously.

I got a fresh Band-Aid and sat down on the couch next to Lily. She carefully began removing the bloody one. Our knees were almost touching and as she bent over my hand her head was within inches and I could smell the scent of her shampoo.

"Stop fidgeting." She playfully tapped my knee.

When she was done I smoothed the new bandage with my fingers. "Thank you."

When she didn't reply I looked up to see her gazing at me with an expression of amusement. "You're dangerous with a knife. You need someone to take care of you."

I tried to think of a witty reply, but none came.

Lily settled back on the couch. "Did you know that Alan got into more trouble Friday night?"

"Terri told me. She always seems to be up on all the news."

"Terri?" Lily knit her brow. "Oh yes, the horn player. Vickie's upset. When she came here she began using her graduate students to assist with the community orchestra but Alan's rich old uncle gave the college a sizable donation and there was hope he would leave more in his will so Vickie was almost forced to take Alan as her assistant. We all know his limitations as a conductor but there's something else. Vickie's never one to be intimidated by anyone but she once told me that Alan frightens her. The uncle did die and left more money to the college so Vickie had to keep him on. Now, she finally has a reason to get rid of him but unfortunately we only have a few weeks of the season left."

"Terri told me that Katy, the other horn player, went

out with him but he scared her too. Amy Leland, the horn player that disappeared, dated him to get the first chair and then dumped him."

Lily looked uncomfortable. "That was an unpleasant situation for Vickie." She clearly did not want to discuss it further.

I made the sandwiches, carried them into the living room with the coffee and sat down on the couch. "I don't care for this couch. It's not an antique or anything special and it's so uncomfortable." The couch was covered in a gaudy floral print. "I like the leather couch you have in your living room."

Lily looked around the room. "Yes, I think it would go well in here."

We finished our meal. As I got Lily's jacket from the closet and we stood in the hallway I briefly thought how wonderful it would be if she was living here and didn't have to leave.

"Thanks for the pleasant evening and for the Irish flute CD."

I grinned. "Better wait until you listen to it."

I watched as she drove away wondering what she meant when she said her couch would go well in my living room.

CHAPTER TWENTY-TWO

I was leaving the campus on a cold, sunny April afternoon, walking along and thinking about the plant pathogens we had just covered in my class, when I heard someone call my name.

I turned to see Vickie in a black wool coat with a gold-patterned designer scarf around her neck. She shifted the briefcase in her gloved hand and hurried to catch up to me. "Finished for the day?"

"Yes, I was just heading home." I adjusted the briefcase strap over my shoulder and stuffed my hands in the pockets of my peacoat. I had left my gloves in the Jeep.

"Come over to my house. I make a good martini. Oh, that's right, you don't like them. Well, I have some good wine."

I hesitated. "I'm not sure if…"

"Come on, we can discuss the upcoming concert."

It wasn't that I didn't want to go to Vickie's house but I was not interested in getting involved with her. Attractive as she was, she was too much for me. On the other hand I didn't want to turn down the invitation to discuss the concert and just enjoy the company of our orchestra's conductor.

I looked at my watch. "I guess I could come for a short time."

When I arrived and parked in front of Vickie's home she was in the driveway waiting as her garage door rose majestically to admit her SUV.

Her house was a large red brick Colonial with black shutters and a brick path leading to the front entrance. The shrubs along the front of the house were starting to grow up over the windows, and I could see a long row of towering arbor vitae lining both sides of her lot separating her from the neighbors. Other huge trees swayed in the breeze above the house in the backyard.

Vickie unlocked the side door. I followed her into the kitchen where she threw her purse and briefcase onto a chair. The kitchen, with two large windows, could have been light and airy but the trees in the back had taken over and shaded the room.

"I just had these granite countertops installed." Vickie took my jacket and gestured toward some handsome-looking counters. I wondered how they would look in my kitchen, replacing the Formica.

"Come into the living room." Vickie led the way.

The large room had the look of a professionally decorated space. A beautiful Oriental carpet in muted colors over the hardwood floor, furniture artfully arranged around the fireplace, original-looking oil paintings on the wall and over the fireplace a hunting scene, and two Staffordshire dogs on the mantel. There was an absence of the knickknacks and collections that tended to clutter a room but books and magazines piled on the floor next to the chairs and on the coffee table diminished the designer effect. Papers and music were strewn around and in the corner stood a lovely baby grand piano covered with scores and stray pieces of music. I thought of the baby grand I wanted to buy.

Vickie adjusted the thermostat on the wall and then walked over to a small but expensive Sony sound system. I had thought about buying a similar one and priced it after I moved here. She selected a CD and put it in.

"Bach, *Goldberg Variations*, I'm not in the mood for anything orchestral. Do you like white or red wine?"

"I prefer white, but red is fine."

"Don't worry, I have both." Vickie disappeared into the kitchen. I could hear the clinking of glasses and the refrigerator door opening and closing while Vickie hummed to the Bach.

I sat in a chair across the room. One where I didn't have to displace anything.

Vickie entered the room carrying a martini glass and a wineglass. She swept some papers aside on the glass-topped coffee table in front of the couch and put down the glasses.

"Come over here, don't sit across the room." She picked up some books and dropped them on the floor in front of the elegant couch. "Just a minute, I have some cheese and crackers."

She returned with a handful of cocktail napkins imprinted with notes and treble clefs and a large crystal plate containing several kinds of cheese and crackers. She sat down, picked up her martini, crossed her legs and leaned back.

I gingerly sipped my wine. Since I had been invited to discuss the upcoming concert, I began, "I think our soloist is excellent."

"Yes, he's talented, a little bit of a showoff, but I don't think we will have a repeat of the problem with the last one."

"Your new assistant is great. Everyone in the orchestra likes her."

Vickie took a long sip of her martini. "Yes, Allie is very capable; I wish I could have had her assisting us earlier. Now she's graduating, so she won't be back."

"I heard the Kalinnikov is going to draw a large audience for the concert. Very few have ever heard it performed live."

Vickie drained her glass. "I hope they appreciate it. It took a lot of work to get this orchestra up to playing it. Of course you're doing a fine job. Probably better than Karen."

"Oh, I don't think that. She…"

Vickie rose and went into the kitchen returning with another martini and the wine bottle. She filled my glass, sat down and reached back releasing the barrette holding her long thick hair, letting it fall down around her shoulders.

"Have something to eat." She leaned forward and selected a small cracker. "Enough of the orchestra. I'll be glad when this concert is over." Another sip of her martini. "Do you go to Milwaukee often? To see anyone special?"

"I go occasionally but I'm pretty involved with my classes here."

"How do you like being a student again?"

Before I could formulate an answer Vickie jerked as if she heard something, jumped up, and went to the front window and carefully pulled the drape a few inches back to look out. Then she came back and sat down on the couch.

"Julie, I'm worried. I think Alan has been stalking me."

I wasn't sure how to reply. "What makes you think that?"

Vickie picked up her glass and looked toward the window. "He has a white van and several nights now I've noticed it on the street in front of my house. A couple of times a white van followed me home."

"Have you reported him to the police?"

Vickie waved her hand. "How could I? The city is full of white vans."

"What about his license plate number?"

"The one time I saw it, it was covered with mud. Maybe I should look for some identifying features." She paused and looked down into her glass. "He's so sick."

I was worried for Vickie. What if Alan was really after her? From what I'd heard about him it might be true. I tried to steer the conversation back to the orchestra just to get her mind off her fear.

"I know this is in the future but do you have a concert program planned for the fall?"

"I can't plan that far ahead right now." Vickie picked up the wine bottle, added more to my glass and then carried her glass to the kitchen.

I desperately tried to think how I could end the evening. Vickie returned with a fresh martini, flopped down on the couch and studied me. "Are you and Lily close?"

"I know her from the orchestra."

Vickie sipped her martini and let the subject drop. "This town is so restricting," she complained. "Everyone knows everyone else and what he or she is doing. I've had enough. How could you move up here?"

"I've only been here about ten months and I'm busy with my classes and my house." I added, "The orchestra has been wonderful for me."

Vickie yawned. I knew this was my time to escape.

I threw down the remainder of my wine and stood up examining my watch.

"Thank you so much, I've enjoyed this but I better get going."

Vickie looked resigned. "Okay, Julie." She got my jacket, led me to the front door and then put her hand on my arm to stop me.

"Wait, is there a white van out there?" She gripped my arm and I could feel her breath on my cheek.

I peered down the street. "I don't see one." She released her grip on my arm. I turned back to her. "Thanks Vickie."

"Bye Julie." She closed the door.

All the way home I watched in my rearview mirror for a white van. I hoped Vickie was not in trouble. If she was, how could I help her?

CHAPTER TWENTY-THREE

Friday, the night of the dress rehearsal for our Sunday concert, had arrived. A dress rehearsal did not imply dressing in performance dress but was merely a final performance where the orchestra ran through the entire program as if there were an audience. Most of us were wearing jeans and sweaters or T-shirts.

As I entered Stofer Hall Joanne was helping her daughter wheel in her harp so I held the door for them and then made my way to the horn section.

My source of news, Terri, had information on a new development.

"Guess what?" She looked around her. "They're afraid Alan is going to make a scene at the concert Sunday so the campus security is going to be there."

This is all we need, I thought, with the larger than usual turnout and my nervousness about my part in the Kalinnikov.

The woman called in to play fourth horn joined us. Vickie had given her the parts earlier in the week so she could practice them. Thin, with a wiry body and short gray hair, she very graciously shook our hands, introduced herself as Agnes and then took her place at the end of the section.

After rehearsing the "Egmont Overture" and the Weber concertino we took a break and I looked for Lily but saw she was deep in conversation with the first oboe player, who had joined the orchestra in January. Once, Lily looked up, saw me and waved but the break ended before I had a chance to go over and talk to her.

The Kalinnikov went fairly well and the new addition to our horn section did a capable job with her part. The dress rehearsal ran late and when it was over everyone was tired and ready to pack up and go right home. I emptied my horn, put it away and went to join Lily who was carefully swabbing out her flute. She waved goodnight to the oboe player who stood up, nodded and left, ignoring me.

"Julie, Jackie was telling me that she and her friend want to go to the new brew pub after the concert Sunday. She's asked us to join them. It turns out her friend is also on the faculty here, a professor in the history department. I think they live together. What do you think? Should we join them?"

I assumed the woman with the short dark hair who had just left was Jackie the oboe player. "If you want to. It's fine with me."

"Great. By the way, I heard they're expecting a big audience for the concert."

"I don't want to alarm you but Terri told me the campus security is going to be there because they think Alan might cause some kind of trouble. And Vickie thinks he's stalking her."

Lily didn't ask when or where I learned this about Vickie but frowned and shook her head. "Oh I hope not. He's turned out to be a real problem."

We said goodnight in the parking lot and as I drove home I realized with dismay that now that our rehearsals were over until fall, I would no longer be assured of seeing Lily every Monday night.

Sunday morning I went for a short run, not just for the exercise but to help calm my nerves before the concert. Most of the snow had melted and although the day was overcast no further snow was predicted.

I ran for about an hour and then as I turned to come down the block to my house the sun appeared and I heard a birdcall. I looked up into a large maple tree and there it was. A robin. I couldn't wait to tell Lily.

***

I made my way through the noisy crowd entering Stofer Hall and to the room where we orchestra members left our coats and instrument cases. Removing my coat I took my horn from its case. I was wearing full black slacks and a long-sleeved black silk blouse with a mandarin collar. An outfit I had worn before with my orchestra in Milwaukee.

Several of the musicians were visiting and were occupied oiling valves and applying rosin to their bows. In a corner I saw Jackie, the oboe player, working on her reed. I was glad I didn't play an instrument that was dependent on the fickleness of a piece of cane.

One of the younger trumpet players, evidently unaccustomed to dressing up, was tugging nervously at his tie, and a trombone player was trying, without success, to brush pet fur off his pants. The clarinet player with the frizzy hair stood in the center of the room, a reed sticking out of her mouth. She was wearing a black ensemble that resembled a pair of lounge pajamas.

I picked up my folder of music and went down the hall to the stage. I was usually early but this afternoon Terri and Katy were already there, and Agnes arrived a few minutes later.

Agnes leaned over. "My son and his family are all here. They are so excited." She pointed toward the audience.

Katy added, "My sister and some of her friends who never go to symphony concerts heard what a big event this is, and came to see me. We're all going out afterward."

Terri, who was playing scales, put her horn down. "My parents come to every concert but they said this one is special."

The seven hundred seats of the hall were filling to capacity. Music majors at the college, who served as ushers, were busily handing out programs and showing the audience to their seats. Even our concerts in Milwaukee didn't attract crowds this large.

When Lily came onstage carrying her music and silver flute I was struck again by how lovely she was. She was wearing the same revealing top as the last concert. I remembered the first time I saw her in the Continuing Education office and how I felt when she smiled at me. Now, before she sat down she looked my way with the same smile. Even though our season was over and it was possible I would see very little of her, I was determined to pursue our friendship.

The concert began. Allie came onstage, acknowledged the scattered applause and called for an A from the oboe.

The various instruments sounded their tuning note and then settled down in silence waiting for Allie to give the downbeat.

The audience loved the "Egmont Overture." As the triumphant last notes sounded they broke into applause and Allie took two bows.

Then Vickie came to the podium preceded by our soloist. Vickie looked elegant in a long black skirt and black velvet top. Where Allie was capable, Vickie had a commanding presence. More tuning, a moment of silence and then we launched into the Weber Clarinet Concertino. The young soloist performed flawlessly, with virtuosity and musicality. His friends and family bolstered the applause following his performance.

At the intermission I met up with Lily. She put her hand on my arm and lowered her voice. "Don't be nervous. You will be wonderful in the Kalinnikov, I know from the rehearsals. Don't forget, we do this for our own enjoyment."

The lights dimmed and the intermission was over. Vickie strode onto the stage and the moment most of the audience came for had arrived. I took several deep breaths to calm my nerves.

Once I played the opening phrase of the Kalinnikov I forgot everything but the music. All the weeks of practice fell into place and I could only think of how much I loved the parts I was playing. Everyone around me played with the same intensity.

The second movement with the ethereal harp solo captivated the audience and after the powerful, forceful ending they burst into loud applause. Vickie gestured for the individual sections to rise and take a bow, the horns first.

Afterward, in the reception room, Vickie approached me and put her hand on my shoulder. "Magnificent playing, Julie." She turned to the other three women. "And the rest of the horn section."

I answered for all of us. "Thank you, Professor, we enjoyed it but everyone in the orchestra played so well." Six months ago I would have been thrilled by her words and the touch of her hand. Now, I looked anxiously across the room. Lily was standing there smiling at me.

"Excuse me." I hurried over to her.

"Wonderful job, Julie." She was beaming. "Should we go over to the brew pub? I can meet you there."

As we walked out I saw Vickie standing in the center of the room. There was a large crowd gathered around her, including Marty from Tosca, who was standing with a handsome man I assumed was her husband. He looked like the one I had imagined with Lily. Vickie ignored them as she watched us leave together.

When Lily and I entered the Green River Brew Pub she indicated two women seated at a table across the room. "There they are."

One of them, Jackie the oboe player, waved to us and we made our way through the crowd. As we took off our coats and sat down Jackie introduced us to her friend Vivian. I shook hands with a thin woman with medium-length brown hair showing touches of gray. She appeared older than Jackie but had a pleasant, intelligent face. As soon as we had placed our drink orders with the eager young man who waited on us, Lily and Vivian began talking together about their experiences teaching at the college.

"You look as if you enjoy sports. What do you like?" Jackie's abrupt question took me by surprise.

"I run, bike, snowshoe and cross-country ski. I guess I like the silent sports."

"Do you canoe?"

"I only did that once. I sat in front where I didn't have to do too much."

Jackie took a sip of her beer, some special brew she had asked a lot of questions about before ordering. "Vivian and I have a cottage on a small lake not too far from here. They don't allow motors but we have a canoe. It's very enjoyable. Maybe you and Lily would like to come out this summer."

"That would be fun, and I could get a canoe if you show me how to steer it."

At this point we both looked across the table where Lily and Vivian were giggling together over some incident at a faculty meeting.

Jackie turned back to me. "What happened to that assistant conductor, what's his name, Alan?"

"He got in trouble in a barroom fight, twice actually. Vickie had enough."

"Vickie? Oh, Professor Read. I don't know why she hired him in the first place. He was a terrible conductor."

I explained, and added, "She didn't have a choice."

Jackie nodded. "I get it. What do you do?"

"I'm a student at Northbrook in the horticulture program. I have a biology degree but want to go into plant pathology. What about you?"

"I teach high school math and German. This fall I got a position up here. I was teaching in Appleton and came up here on weekends and vacations to see Vivian. She owns a home, and I live with her now."

I thought of my aunt's visits and trips with Laura Gorman when they both had time off from their teaching jobs.

The meal passed enjoyably. Jackie became friendlier, maybe deciding I was all right, and Lily and Vivian had their jobs at Northbrook College to talk about.

In the parking lot we waved goodbye as they drove off in Jackie's red Firebird.

"Jackie invited us to their cottage this summer," I told Lily. "How do you feel about canoeing?"

"I'm not against it." Lily laughed. "Seriously, I think

it would be fun, probably good exercise too. Julie, you did a lovely job on the concert today. I imagine you are exhausted. Go get some rest, I'll call you."

I stood next to my Jeep and waved as she drove off.

CHAPTER TWENTY-FOUR

Saturday morning I was up early waiting for my coffeemaker to finish dripping, the rich aroma of the coffee filling my kitchen. The furnace blew pleasingly warm air into the room as I looked out the window at my thermometer. After a light snowfall overnight the temperature had dropped and although this was mid-April it was in the twenties. I decided to go for a run after my coffee and before breakfast while the snow was still fresh and clean and the air clear and cold.

I ran for about an hour and then headed home. Two days earlier Lily had called me about going to the bicycle shop and was coming over in the afternoon.

Back home, I heard the bang of the mail slot flap in the door. Three pieces of mail lay on the front hall floor.

I picked up and examined a utility bill, an advertisement for carpet cleaning and a fat business-size envelope addressed to me in a large wavering hand. The return label, imprinted with an American flag, read June Gorman. I took the mail to my newly created office and slit open June's envelope. Inside was a newspaper clipping and a note written on a piece of stationery decorated with roses.

I sat down to decipher June's note. She wrote how shocked and saddened they were when Laura Gorman's body was found. There would be a brief memorial service at the Lutheran church on Monday. I unfolded the newspaper clipping and read the article. An old dam had been removed a week ago and when the water level in the pond fell a car was discovered. Inside was a body and although it was nearly thirty years old the license plate had been traced to Laura Gorman. A relative recalled she had disappeared after leaving for a grocery shopping trip. It had been raining that day and it was thought that her car had skidded off the road into the pond and gone undiscovered all these years despite efforts by the local police to locate her.

I laid the note and article on my desk. How sad for Laura, and for my aunt who must have always hoped Laura would reappear some day.

I went to the phone and ordered flowers for the memorial service then changed it to a large plant, something June could take home and keep.

In the living room I knelt down and arranged some logs in the fireplace and then lit a fire. It was still cold enough to light a fire but this would be the last one of the season.

In the basement I opened the old leather suitcase and took out the bundles of letters. The suitcase would go out for the trash next week. I didn't want to look at it again. I carried the letters upstairs and laid them on the floor in front of the fireplace.

As I was sitting on the living room floor watching the flames, the doorbell rang. When I opened the door Lily was standing there smiling. "Hi Julie, I'm not too early am I?"

"No, not at all." I stepped aside to let her in.

She looked into the living room. "You have a fire going. It looks so pleasant but is it that cold?"

I took her jacket, and she laid her purse on a chair. "I'm going to burn something." Lily looked puzzled. "Sit down, I want to show you something."

I went to my desk, brought back June's letter with the newspaper article and handed them to Lily. I waited while Lily held the papers in her lap and leaned over to read them, her dark hair falling across her face. She put down the letter then picked up the newspaper article. When she had finished she sat silently and then looked over at me with a look of concern.

"This is terrible. What a tragic ending to your aunt's relationship with Laura." She looked toward the fireplace. "Are those the letters?"

"Yes, I'm going to burn them." I stood up, walked over and sat on the floor next to the fireplace. Lily sat next to me.

As I removed the red ribbon from around a bundle of letters Lily leaned forward, reached out, and placed her hand on mine. "Julie, wait. I think we should preserve these letters, at least for now." She hesitated. "They represent the love Laura had for your aunt." She removed her hand. "Perhaps we could read them together some day."

I looked down at the letters as the heat of the flames warmed my face. "Of course. You're right." Lily was near me on the floor with her arms around her knees as she gazed into the flames.

We sat in silence and then Lily looked up at me. "Julie, I've been thinking about how brief life can be and perhaps if I love someone I should do something about it."

I fumbled with the letters in dismay. Had she met someone? Could it be a man like the one I pictured her with when I first saw her?

Lily continued to watch the fire. "The first year I came to the college I had a relationship with Vickie. At first it was wonderful, although Vickie could be demanding. One evening she called me to come over to her house. I had a project, which had to be completed by the next day, so I explained that I had to stay home and finish it. She was angry and hung up on me. I was done with the work earlier than I had expected so I drove over to Vickie's house to surprise her."

I sat in stunned silence unable to take my eyes from her face as Lily continued. "At first she didn't answer the door and when she did she was in her robe and acted uncomfortable. I thought she had just decided to go to bed early. Then a woman came out of her bedroom wearing a pajama top. It was the horn player Amy."

I crushed the letters in my hand and waited for Lily to continue.

"I was so hurt and humiliated that I vowed not to get involved with anyone again." She turned to me. "I was attracted to you the first time I saw you in the Continuing Education Office. Then in the orchestra when I realized you were a horn player I thought you might be another one like Amy, and Vickie seemed to be interested in you."

"Lily, she did make a pass at me but as much as I admire her I wasn't interested. Only in you."

"Julie, I love you. Come here." She reached out to me and we held each other, our bodies closely, fiercely together.

She moved her hands to cup my face and our lips met in a soft tentative kiss, which became more urgent as we experienced the long awaited pleasure of sharing our first kiss. Lily took the sleeve of my shirt in her fingers and tugged lightly. "Take your clothes off," she whispered.

My hands were trembling as I fumbled with the buttons of my shirt while Lily pulled her sweater over her head and undid her bra. She finished unbuttoning my shirt and moved it off my shoulders. I had nothing on underneath and when our bodies came together I felt the exquisite pleasure of her breasts against mine.

Struggling out of our jeans, we kissed again, more deeply and passionately. She pushed me down to the carpet, our bodies close together.

I buried my face in her hair inhaling the familiar scent, kissed her cheek and moved my lips to hers for another tender kiss. "Oh Lily, why did I wait so long? It seems I've wanted you forever."

"I was so afraid."

Her body was even lovelier than I had imagined and now we were sharing the pleasures of touches and caresses.

I gently traced her face and throat with my fingertips. I couldn't get enough of her. I ran my fingertips lightly down her body to her full, firm breasts. She pulled my mouth down to them and I felt her body stiffen as my lips closed around a nipple. As I slid my hand down her body she took my hand in hers guiding it between her thighs. "Do you want me…inside?"

"Yes, please."

Our bodies melted, arched together and Lily cried out, as the letters lay scattered around us.

***

Upstairs in my bed as we lay tangled in the sheets I sat up abruptly.

"We never got to the bicycle shop."

Lily stretched her arms over her head. "Oh, don't worry, they'll still have one for me. Say those things you said to me before."

I grinned. "You mean about what kind of a bicycle to buy?"

Lily grabbed my arm and pulled me down. "No, silly, you know what I mean."

"Lily, there is something I forgot to tell you."

She paused and looked anxiously at me.

"I saw a robin last week."

Lily smiled. "How sweet. That must mean spring is coming." Then she asked. "When did you first feel that you loved me?"

I didn't hesitate. "The day I saw you in the Continuing Education Office. You were so lovely and when you smiled at me I was, as they say, smitten." I hesitated. "But then I thought you were probably married to a handsome successful man and with two perfect children."

Lily laughed. "I don't think so."

I asked. "What about you?"

Lily pondered the question. "I think it was on Christmas Eve when you told me how rich you were."

"What if I told you I lost my money in the stock market?"

"We could get along together on my salary."

"I still have all the money."

We both laughed and Lily embraced me and pulled me down on top of her, holding me tightly against her body. A shudder ran through me as she lightly stroked my back with her fingertips and pressed her lips against my throat. She closed her eyes and murmured. "Julie, my dear heiress."

As a lover Lily was everything I had imagined she would be, and I have to admit that I don't think I disappointed her.

CHAPTER TWENTY-FIVE

I was drinking my early morning coffee and waiting for my toast to pop up from the toaster when the phone rang.

"Julie, glad I got you. I hope I'm not calling you too early."

Then I recognized the voice. "Beth, how are you?"

"Fine. Listen Julie, I'm coming up there today to meet with a detective about Amy. I want them to reopen the case and finally find out what happened to her."

Beth's voice was anxious and determined. "I thought we could meet for an early lunch so you could go over with me the people Amy knew when she lived up there."

"I'm sorry Beth, I have classes all day."

"Oh, you still do that."

"Beth, I don't think I could add too much more. I told you everything I learned."

Beth forged ahead. "They say she was an adult when she disappeared and there was no sign of foul play but I'm going to insist they follow up on everyone she had any..." Beth faltered. "Any association with."

There wasn't anything more to say to Beth. "I'm sorry I can't meet with you. I've told you everything I know. Keep in touch, let me know what they tell you."

"Yes, sure. Bye Julie."

***

I was busy with my classes all that day but the next morning as I sat in the lab peering into my microscope I began to realize what might happen.

If they took Beth seriously and did pursue the case they might find out that Amy had had an affair with Vickie. I adjusted the focus on my microscope and considered that if they knew Vickie had cheated on Lily with Amy, and if Lily had found out, she might be suspected of retaliating against Amy.

I made some notes, looked up from my microscope and then put my pen down. I had long ago lost interest in what had happened to Amy. In addition to being an unlikeable person, the fact was that everyone I talked with believed she had just up and left town. But now the person in trouble might be Lily. I had to do something.

I knew there had been some trouble between Vickie and Amy. I tried to recall what Vickie had said that afternoon at Tosca when we were drinking martinis. Something like, things had gone wrong. Or was it everything had gone wrong.

I remembered the night Lily had described to me the

oddly shaped fishpond in Vickie's garden. Somehow I had to see it.

My one class ended at noon and as I drove home I began to formulate a plan.

At home I changed into my cargo pants, a denim jacket and work boots. I added my pruners in a holster on my belt and found a baseball cap with a tree logo, something from a seminar on oaks I had attended. Rummaging in the tool drawer in my kitchen I found a metal tape measure. Then I took my clipboard, and looking through the mail piled on my desk, I found a prospectus from one of my investments. It was a thick publication so I tore the front cover off and put it on the clipboard and then put a piece of graph paper from my briefcase on top. A ballpoint pen added to the clip completed it.

As I drove leisurely through Vickie's neighborhood all was quiet. This was an area of professionals who were away pursuing their lucrative occupations during the day.

I tried to justify to myself what I was doing. When Vickie told me everything had gone wrong between her and Amy maybe this meant an argument or even a fight. I had recently seen a television program where a woman pushed her husband during an argument and he fell, hit his head and died. What if this happened to Amy? And Vickie had panicked and buried her in the garden and then maybe even built a crude fishpond over the spot.

I pulled up in front of Vickie's home and got out of the Jeep carrying my clipboard and trying to look briskly professional. As I purposefully strode toward Vickie's backyard a woman emerged from the other side of the tall arbor vitae separating their yards.

"So. She's finally going to have some work done on that garden."

I stopped suddenly, face-to-face with a woman with cropped gray hair and a ruddy complexion. She was dressed in a wool plaid jacket, corduroy pants and sturdy hiking boots.

"Well, perhaps. I'm just here to give an estimate."

She approached closer. "What company are you with?"

Oh no. I thought quickly. "Green Brook Landscaping."

"Never heard of you."

"We're new. Our first season."

She stepped forward. "I might need some work. Give me your brochure and a business card."

"We're so new, they are still at the printer's. But we expect them early next week."

She pushed her hands into the pockets of her jacket. "Well, leave me the literature when you get it."

"I certainly will." I watched as she retreated to her yard. What had I got myself into?

I picked my way through the damp grass and mud to the backyard. The day was cool and sunny but as I entered the garden huge trees blocked the sunlight and the atmosphere changed. I saw an overgrowth of dead plants and decaying vegetation and there under a spindly ash tree was the fishpond. Rotting leaves floated in the murky water and a fallen tree branch covered one end of the long pond.

Somewhere in the distance a dog barked, but here it was silent and desolate. I took my tape measure from my pocket, and kneeling on the damp ground, measured the pond, entered the measurements on my clipboard and then stood up and looked around me. Because of the height of the arbor vitae it didn't appear as if Vickie's neighbor could see her garden, even from her second-floor window. Suddenly I wanted to escape from this cheerless place.

When I reached my Jeep I stood behind it and appeared to jot some notes on my clipboard just in case the neighbor was watching. Actually, I was listing the grocery items I needed to pick up on my way home. Lily was coming over the next evening, Thursday, and had offered to bring Chinese food. Two months ago I had signed up for a workshop at the University Field Station so I would be gone most of the weekend.

Driving away I realized that my theory had been ridiculous. Vickie was not the type to panic in any situation and what if she had returned home early and discovered me poking around in her garden?

In the supermarket parking lot I took off my baseball cap and holster with the pruners, throwing them on the seat next to me with the tape measure and clipboard. Taking a deep breath I lay back in my seat. I had to get a hold of myself. Escapades like this were not going to help Lily.

***

Late Thursday afternoon I arranged the pillows on the couch and straightened the magazines on the table as I anxiously waited for Lily to arrive. Although we had talked on the phone several times, I was filled with excitement and desire as I looked forward to our first meeting since Saturday.

The doorbell rang and I hurried to open the door. Lily stood there holding a large bag, which from the aroma I knew was the Chinese food.

"Hi, Julie, sorry I'm late. They were so busy it took longer than I expected."

We stood there smiling at each other and then I awkwardly took the bag from her and opened the front hall closet. "You can hang your jacket in here, let me take this to the kitchen."

In the kitchen I set the bag on the counter. When I turned around Lily was standing in the doorway with an expression on her face I had not seen before.

"I missed you, come here."

I rushed into her arms and we held each other.

"I'm sorry we couldn't meet sooner, too much going on at school." She pushed the hair away from my eyes. "How has your week been?"

"I missed you too. I couldn't think of anything else but seeing you today."

We kissed and I clung to her. "Should we go upstairs? It's kind of early to eat."

She smiled. "We can heat up the food later."

***

Lily ran her hand down my body. "Did you play sports in school?"

"Basketball. High school and then at the university."

"I bet you were the star."

"No, I was dependable and a pretty fair ball-handler." I laughed. "The coach described me as having a good work ethic."

"Of course, you would."

I kissed her forehead and temple and then ran my hands through her dark hair. "I'm sorry I have to go away this weekend."

"Tell me about it again."

"The field station is about forty miles from here. It's a workshop on Pollination Ecology. I have to leave early Friday morning and then I come back after it ends Sunday morning. I have to take a sleeping bag and towels."

"I don't know what Pollination Ecology is but I'm sure it will be interesting for you. The rest sounds a little primitive."

"Call you when I get back?"

She smiled. "After you have a hot shower. We'll get together Sunday." She pushed her hair back. "Do you ever hear from your friends in Milwaukee?"

"The last time I saw them they were talking about

moving to Florida. I guess they haven't or they would have let me know."

"Are you hungry? Should we heat up the Chinese food?"

I didn't mention that Beth had come to town and called me. It wasn't that I was keeping it from Lily but I doubted if anything would come of Beth's trip, and I was afraid mentioning Amy would bring back unpleasant memories for Lily. I didn't want to do anything to upset her.

I sat up. "Yes, let's attack that food."

CHAPTER TWENTY-SIX

On a sunny day in early May I drove the Jeep into the parking lot of the Green River Nature Center. Carol had called me two days earlier to tell me the Education Center, to be named after my aunt, Margaret Burke, was nearing completion and a dedication date was being planned for sometime in early June. Carol wanted me to see the center and hinted that I should be present for the dedication and perhaps participate in the ribbon cutting.

As I walked up the path I saw a newly built, long, low, wood-and-brick building that was well adapted to the natural site. Carol emerged from the building and hurried toward me wearing a fleece jacket bearing the name and logo of the center and a knit cap over the same senior haircut.

"Julia, so glad you could come to see this building, all thanks to your aunt. We are so thrilled, the dedication is being planned. Oh, come inside."

We entered the nearly completed building and Carol led me through the auditorium, exhibit rooms, art gallery and classrooms. Sunlight poured in the windows and everything was bright and clean with the fresh smell of new building materials.

"We're in the process of moving in some of the exhibits." Carol pointed proudly toward a huge stuffed black bear standing on its hind legs with the arms extended in a menacing pose.

"We've tried to incorporate green building practices." She waved toward the interior. "Natural ventilation, passive solar heating and cooling, the use of recycled materials. Your aunt would be so proud."

I tried in vain to remember any green practices my aunt had applied to her home. But the center was very impressive and I murmured my approval.

When we walked outside Carol pointed to an area several yards away. "We wanted to have a butterfly house here this summer. Do you know what they are?"

"Yes, I do." I had visited the one at the Milwaukee Public Museum.

She sighed. "We just can't raise the funds this year. We had hoped to open it in July. When our massive fund drive for the center fell short we were so grateful for your aunt's legacy. We tried selling engraved bricks for the butterfly house but we just couldn't raise enough."

Carol turned away from the not-to-be butterfly house. "I'm afraid this will have to wait for next year. Such a shame, the children would love it." She hastily added, "And, of course, adults too."

I looked at the empty grassy area. "How much more money do you need for this butterfly house?"

Carol named a figure. It was about the cost of a new baby grand piano.

"If someone donated that amount could they name the butterfly house?"

Carol laughed. "Of course, anything they wanted to name it."

I gestured toward my aunt's new center. "Let's go back inside and talk about this."

***

I had wheeled our bicycles outside my garage and was just finishing pumping up my tires when Lily pulled her car up in front of my house. She came up the driveway waving to me.

"Hi Julie. Oh, I love this bike." She patted her new metallic green Trek hybrid. We had finally gotten over to the bicycle shop to pick it out. For now I was keeping it in my garage.

"Do we need our helmets for riding in the neighborhood?" Lily looked stylish in a running jacket and baseball cap. Actually, she looked good in anything.

"I don't think so." The streets in my neighborhood were quiet and free of traffic, especially on a Sunday morning. The idea was to let Lily become comfortable with her new bicycle and the gear shifting.

We rode up and down the streets and it didn't take long for Lily to become accustomed to the bicycle. As with the snowshoes she was graceful and agile.

After our ride we put the bicycles away in the garage. I told her, "Anytime you want to take your bike home I can bring it over."

"Why would I want to do that? We're going to ride together."

"Well, I just thought if you had other friends to ride with…"

She ruffled my hair. "Let's go inside and get something to drink. I'm really thirsty after all this exercise."

We sat close together on the floral couch in the living room with a glass of wine. Lily's recipe for chicken was baking in the oven. It turned out she liked to cook but found cooking for one not too inspiring.

"Lily, I bought a butterfly house."

She set her glass down. "A what?"

"Do you know what a butterfly house is?"

"Yes, I do. Children love them. But I wasn't sure if I heard you correctly. I don't understand. Is it for your yard?"

"Carol invited me to the Nature Center to see the Margaret Burke Education Center before the dedication in June."

Lily leaned forward listening.

"They wanted to have a butterfly house at the center this summer but couldn't raise the money. So I gave them the money. On the condition they name it as I wanted."

Lily sat back smiling. "The Julia Burke Butterfly House."

"No, Lily. It's to be the Laura Gorman Butterfly House."

"Julie, how wonderful. Both your aunt and her friend will be represented at the Nature Center."

She leaned over and put her arms around me. "I can't believe how generous and thoughtful this is of you."

"Lily, is there something at the Nature Center you want named after you?"

Laughing, we embraced and fell back on the couch together.

CHAPTER TWENTY-SEVEN

As I left my last afternoon class I saw Denise ahead of me in the hall. I called to her.

"Julie, how are you? How are your classes this semester?" Denise looked smart in a tan suede vest and handsome brown cable-knit sweater.

I caught up to her. "Great, what about you?"

"Guess what? I got the job at Northstar Perennial Farms. I've been working in their greenhouses, growing our plants for spring."

"Good for you. Do you like it?"

"I love it, that's what I want to specialize in, greenhouse

production. You know the 1999 Perennial Plant of the Year is Goldsturm Rudbecki, well, we are growing it and it's certain to be a big seller."

I had never seen Denise so enthusiastic. "The black-eyed Susan-type flower? I'll have to get some for my yard. Let's go get a drink. Catch up."

At Dos Amigos, as we were examining our menus, Denise looked up. "You said you were here at this place with the orchestra. Is that the community orchestra you play in?"

"Yes, it is."

"The reason I ask is I heard this guy Alan is a conductor of the orchestra."

"He was only an assistant. How do you know him?"

"One night Mary and I went to a bar to watch a basketball game we couldn't get on our cable channel. This guy was hitting on three women at a table next to us."

This certainly sounded like Alan.

Denise continued. "The women weren't interested and he became belligerent. I said to Mary if he comes over here I'll take care of him."

Denise was slight of build and I thought unless she had some martial arts training it wouldn't have happened.

"The staff couldn't control him and called the police. It ruined everyone's evening." She laid her menu down. "Why would the orchestra want him?"

I explained about his old uncle's donation, and Denise sighed, shook her head and looked back at the menu.

"You know, Denise, Amy went out with him."

She looked up. "What! Why would she do that?"

"From what I was told it was to get a first chair position. He was in charge of the auditions, but once she had it she dropped him."

"That sounds like Amy." Denise looked thoughtful. "We all thought she just left town. What if he had something to do with her disappearance?"

We were interrupted when two women approached the table to talk to Denise. She introduced them but I barely caught their names. They nodded to me and began a discussion with Denise of the spring softball league schedule.

As they debated the pros and cons of the dates and location of the games I wondered about Amy. Besides the universally accepted theory of her leaving town on her own I now had another idea about her disappearance.

***

On a cold, damp evening I sat back on Lily's leather couch relaxing in the warmth of the room and the aroma of her cooking. Lasagna was baking in the oven for our dinner.

Outside a driving rain hit the window and ran down in streams. I was so comfortable in here but nervous because I had something important to ask Lily.

She came from the kitchen area wiping her hands on a dishtowel. Her face was flushed from the heat of the oven, her hair was tied back with a red ribbon and she was wearing a blue work shirt with the sleeves rolled up and several of the top buttons open. She turned, tossed the towel onto the kitchen counter and crossed the room to perch on the arm of the couch. Smoothing my hair she smiled down at me. "I hope you're hungry, dear."

"Lily, I have something I want to talk to you about."

She moved to sit down on the couch next to me with an anxious look on her face. "What is it, Julie? Is something wrong?"

I set my wineglass aside. "Lily, would you ever consider moving in, no, I mean sharing my house with me?"

Lily looked at me wide-eyed. I pressed on. "There are three more bedrooms upstairs, and you could have any of them for anything you want them for."

"Are you sure, Julie?"

"Lily, you know I love you. I've been lonely since I moved here but didn't know why until I met you. Christmas Eve when we were together I wanted you to stay. And then when…"

Lily put her hand on my arm to stop me. "Yes, I would love to. I want us to always be together." She leaned back and looked at me with a twinkle in her eye. "Is this a marriage proposal?"

"It certainly is."

"I accept." She moved closer to me and took my head in her hands kissing me gently as I untied the ribbon in her hair and undid the rest of the buttons on her shirt and slipped it off. My sweatshirt fell to the floor. She wasn't wearing a bra and I moved my lips slowly from her throat to her breasts. Her hands pulled me urgently closer as her breathing quickened.

Later, Lily whispered in my ear, "Can I bring my leather couch?"

We laughed together as the smell of burning lasagna came from the kitchen.

CHAPTER TWENTY-EIGHT

Lily and I were seated opposite one another in a booth at Dos Amigos. Lily ordered a margarita. "I think in a Mexican restaurant that's the drink to order." I agreed and also ordered one.

When the margaritas arrived Lily took a sip then nervously arranged her cutlery.

"I have some news. Today Vickie told me she's resigning."

I waited, not knowing what to say.

"She's accepted a position at a university in upstate New York. It's similar to her position here but they have more funding, better resources, and she will receive a much larger salary."

I was stunned and wasn't sure how I felt, but I had to say something. "Everyone in the orchestra will miss her."

Lily sighed and picked up her drink. "I think this business with Alan took its toll. She seems very excited about the move."

As she spread her napkin in her lap Lily added, "Vickie told me she has a friend she thinks will be an excellent replacement." Lily frowned. "This is between us—her resignation hasn't been announced. I think she said her friend is Sandy Liu. Let's hope she gets the position."

Our food arrived and we both felt we had exhausted the news about Vickie.

Lily picked up her fork. "I think the weather is predicted to be good next weekend when I drive down to Milwaukee."

Lily was attending an all-day symposium at the University of Wisconsin-Milwaukee on Saturday. I had forgotten exactly what the topic was, some esoteric English literature subject, but was happy she would have a chance to get out of town and spend time with her colleagues.

"I'm glad you're staying with your friend. It'd be too late to drive back up here and you won't have to stay at a hotel."

"I haven't seen Mary Ann for almost a year, so I was glad to hear she was attending and that she wanted me to stay with her Saturday night. She lives on the east side so it will be convenient."

Lily pushed some refried beans around on her plate. "Julie, should we take a trip together? We could use a vacation and it would be fun to travel together. We'd have time after summer school."

I looked up eagerly. "I'd love to. Where do you think we should go?"

"I have an idea, let me look into it."

I would go anywhere with Lily. I remembered again the day in the Continuing Education Office when I first saw her and she smiled at me.

"One other thing, I want to buy a new car. I've been putting it off because I dread the dealing it involves. After this winter I feel I have to go ahead."

"After our vacation we'll do some research and go looking." I smiled. "Don't worry, we won't let the dealers get the best of us."

**

Tuesday when I came home from school I found a message on my answering machine.

"Hi Julie, this is Cindy. We're coming up to Green Bay Sunday. Ginger wants to go to the Packer Hall of Fame and we thought maybe you could meet us somewhere. Give me a call."

I wasn't especially anxious to go to the Packer Hall of Fame but did want to see Ginger and Cindy and had an idea for us to get together.

I picked up my mail from the front hall floor and carried it to my desk. On top I saw a letter from the field station and eagerly opened it. I had been accepted for an internship this summer. I couldn't wait to tell Lily as she had encouraged me to apply. I excitedly read the letter again. It would be a busy summer, so unlike my first one here. Then I had been suffering from the aftermath of the fire in the lab and had moved here not knowing anyone. My time had been spent alone driving around exploring my new town.

The other piece of mail was the summer newsletter from the Green River Nature Center. A large part of it was devoted to the upcoming dedication and opening of the Margaret Burke Education Center. Inside was an article headed "Butterfly House To Open." According to the article, the house was to be named the Laura Gorman Butterfly House after a good friend of Margaret Burke who often visited Green River and the Nature Center. She had enjoyed the center so much that she had once expressed a wish to be able to do something for them. This was a slight fantasy of mine, but who knew? It might have happened. Knowing Carol, I doubted if the donor of the butterfly house would remain totally anonymous.

I set my mail aside and sat down to call Cindy. She answered on the third ring. "Julie, you got my message. We're driving up Sunday morning and then back in the late afternoon. Can we get together?"

"Cindy, why don't you come to my house on Saturday? We can go out to eat somewhere, see my town and you stay with me. Then Sunday morning you can go to Green Bay. It's a short drive."

"Sounds great, see you."

Late Saturday afternoon I saw Cindy's silver Mustang pull into my driveway. I grabbed my jacket and went out to meet them.

They stood looking over at my house. Cindy shook her head. "Julie, when we heard you inherited your aunt's house we thought it probably was a little bungalow or a modest ranch house. This is beautiful. A regular mansion."

Ginger picked up the bags and we went in the back door.

In the bedroom opposite mine Lily had already begun moving in her things, so I put them in one of the back bedrooms overlooking the expansive backyard.

"There's a small bathroom up here." I pointed down the hall. "Take your time."

When Ginger and Cindy came down they both stood awkwardly looking around. I thought maybe a drink would lighten up things, plus I had some news for them. "Come into the kitchen and see what you want to drink."

Ginger picked out a bottle of a local beer and Cindy

and I had a glass of wine. Settled in the living room, they began to relax. I said, "I have something to tell you. I'm not going to be living here alone any longer. Lily is moving in and we're going to share a home."

Ginger interrupted, "Julie, you found somebody!"

Cindy smiled knowingly. "I bet it's the professor you told me about. Lily, such a lovely name."

Ginger asked, "Are you in love with her?"

"Very much. She'd be here today but she's in Milwaukee for a seminar."

"How glad we are for you." Ginger raised her beer bottle and we all toasted my happiness.

"What happened about Florida?" I asked them.

Cindy sighed and set her glass down on a strategically placed coaster on the inlaid end table, a souvenir of one of my aunt's trips to Italy.

"We have vacation scheduled for the end of July, and we plan to go down there and seriously look around. We want to get out of here before winter. We heard from Nicole, you remember her, she loves it there and is urging us to move down."

"Any sighting of Amy?"

Cindy laughed. "She didn't mention seeing her. But it's a big state. That reminds me, Beth said she came up here to talk to some detective about reopening Amy's case. She seemed miffed that you couldn't drop everything to meet her."

"There wasn't anything new to tell her."

Much as I didn't want to hear about the lab I had to ask. "How's work going?"

Ginger made a face. "The place is getting worse by the day, and we think there's a chance they're going to lose the lawsuit. Time to get out."

I picked up my glass and took a drink of my wine. "What do you think? Chinese or Mexican?" I didn't think they would like Tosca.

Cindy, who had been looking over the furniture, emptied her glass. "Chinese sounds good to me." Ginger agreed.

On the way to dinner I took them out to show them the town and Northbrook College. I drove to Vickie's neighborhood where the homes were expensive and impressive. Cindy leaned forward from the backseat. "There must be money in this town, look at these houses."

As we drove down Vickie's street I looked ahead to her house and there, driving slowly past her house, was a white van. As I approached the van sped away.

Ginger pointed to it. "Look at that jerk."

Vickie's garage door was closed and there was a light on in the living room but since the drapes were closed I couldn't tell if she was home.

"I think I know who was driving that van. I'll tell you in the restaurant."

The Jade Palace had added some dramatic architectural features such as fancy gold trim and soaring rooflines in an attempt to simulate a Chinese palace. The heavy red front door had a huge iron ring to pull it open, always a challenge for me. Ginger opened it easily.

As we ate our appetizers I told them, "We have this fellow, Alan, who was the assistant conductor of our orchestra. He got in a fight in two different bars for harassing women and was arrested. Our conductor, Professor Read, dismissed him just before our concert and he's angry about it. Now she thinks he's stalking her and that looked like his van in front of her house tonight."

"Is he a problem for you too, Julie?" Ginger leaned forward with a look of concern.

"No, he isn't interested in me."

"Is Lily in danger from him?"

"No, he's only after Professor Read."

"If he came in here I could handle him."

Unlike Denise, Ginger probably could. She had been

attending tae kwon do classes for the last three years and was some color belt, I couldn't remember which one. And besides, he wouldn't be likely to come into the Jade Palace as they only had a service bar.

"There's something else. Amy dated him briefly when she came to town. According to another horn player it was only to win the audition for first horn and then she dropped him."

Cindy speared a piece of egg roll. "Certainly sounds like Amy."

The food was a success, and I insisted on paying the bill. When we got home everyone was too full and too tired for more drinking. After some further conversation about the town and the restaurant we all went to bed.

The next morning, while we ate breakfast, Cindy buttered a muffin and offered, "Julie, I understand why you're happy here. Beautiful house and a pretty nice town." She added, "And now mystery and romance."

Ginger nodded. "You have to let us know about this guy Alan. But be careful, Julie." She looked at her watch. "After the Hall of Fame we're going to eat at Curley's Pub, it's right there at the stadium."

They drove off amidst thanks and promises to keep in touch. As I walked back to the house I looked up at the sky. The day was cool and overcast but no rain was predicted. It was a good day for traveling. My thoughts turned to Lily. She wouldn't be home yet but I looked forward to her call tonight.

CHAPTER TWENTY-NINE

I was out in the yard dragging a fallen tree limb to the curb when I looked over and saw my neighbor Dorothy Rollins drive her clean shiny Buick into her driveway. She saw me, waved and walked over.

"That's a huge branch." She eyed my oak tree. "Good thing it didn't fall on anything."

This was a chance to ask Dorothy about air-conditioning. "Do you know of a good heating and air-conditioning company? I want to replace the furnace and add central air."

"I certainly do. Rodgers Brothers. Eight years ago they

installed my air-conditioning. I tried to persuade your aunt to have it installed, but she wasn't interested. Certainly her house must have been hot in the summer."

"Well, she slept downstairs so maybe she felt she didn't need it."

"Do call Rodgers Brothers. By the way, who is the attractive woman I see visiting you? She looks vaguely familiar."

"She's an English professor at the college. She's going to be moving in with me. Share my home." I didn't bother with some excuse about me having so much room or Lily living in a small apartment.

"Now I know where I saw her. She gave a talk to my women's club on Emily Dickinson. This was about two years ago. It was very interesting. Everyone enjoyed it. Your aunt used to have a friend who visited her. I think she was from Michigan. I don't know what happened to her. I haven't seen her in years."

I decided I just didn't want to go into the Laura Gorman story. "I don't remember. I must have been very young. We didn't visit my aunt too often."

Dorothy nodded knowingly. "I believe there was always some friction between your mother and your aunt."

I searched for a subject to take Dorothy's mind off of my family dynamics. "Where's Pepe? I haven't seen him lately."

Dorothy's face assumed a melancholy expression. "Gone. Just before Christmas, he was twelve, it was kidney failure."

Wrong subject. "I'm sorry to hear that."

Dorothy's face brightened. "I'm getting another, but not until next month when the weather is better." She looked up. "I hope that oak tree is all right." She turned and started back to her car.

As I walked back to the house I wondered how Lily felt about pets. It was a subject we had never discussed. I knew some people disliked all pets while others only liked big dogs or fat ill-tempered longhaired cats.

I was looking in the refrigerator for something to eat when the phone rang.

"Hi Julie, I have a couple of minutes before my first appointment." Lily was going to be working late in her office meeting with students. "What have you been doing?"

"I just came back from talking with my neighbor, Dorothy. She gave me the name of a heating and air conditioning company that she recommends."

"That's good. What's new with her?"

"Her Chihuahua Pepe died in December."

"Oh, how sad."

"She's going to get another one. Another Pepe or Jose." I paused. "Lily, how do you feel about pets?"

"Pets? I haven't had one since I was a child."

"Do you like dogs or cats?"

"I like them both. Dogs are good company and nice to take for walks, great exercise. But for a busy person cats are less demanding. They don't have to be taken out. I guess I would go for a cat, especially if she would sit on my lap. Why do you ask? Are you thinking of getting a pet?"

"No, we have too much going on right now." Maybe in the future, but we would choose it together.

There was a noise in the background. "I have to go, Julie. My first student is here. Talk to you tomorrow. Have a nice evening."

After I hung up I thought some more about having a pet. A cat would be a good choice but I would talk to Lily about adopting an adult cat from the local shelter. Once, in Milwaukee, on a visit to the shelter with friends I had seen the older cats, bewildered and frightened at being confined to a cage in a strange place.

It was only four thirty so I decided to go out for a run. The day was overcast but most of our snow had melted and I wanted to get outdoors. The evening without Lily stretched ahead, and I wasn't sure what to have for dinner or what I would do. Maybe read my new book on the history of poisonous plants.

When I got home from my run it was still light out. The days were definitely getting longer and spring was here.

I was getting ready for my shower when the phone rang. I thought about letting the answering machine get it but curiosity prevailed.

"Julie, my last appointment canceled and I wondered if you've eaten yet."

"No. Can you come over?"

"Yes, see you."

I stepped into the shower looking forward with pleasure to an evening with Lily.

CHAPTER THIRTY

Denise and I met in the hall after leaving our classes.

"Are you done for the day, Julie? I'll walk to the parking lot with you."

She was carrying a notebook, two textbooks and a piece of a tree branch. "I have to go to the farms now." She added excitedly, "We're so busy, actually this is our busiest time of the year."

Denise appeared happy about her new job and unlike her previous job at the garden center she was already displaying pride in her new employer. I was sure they got a dedicated hard-working employee.

When we emerged from the Newton Science Building a light drizzle was falling. Denise turned up the collar on her Windbreaker. "Remember that guy Alan we were talking about?"

"Sure."

"You know Mary works at City Hall. Well, the police station is right next door and she knows some of the women that work there. They told Mary what a problem he's been for the police and that he was overheard in a bar threatening to get even with Northbrook College over some job he didn't get."

"Professor Read is leaving so it's probably the job conducting the community orchestra."

Denise shifted her books. "No, I think the job was Professor Read's at the college."

"That can't be. He has no qualifications for that position. That's totally unrealistic."

Denise laughed. "Who said he was in touch with reality."

We reached the parking lot and Denise pulled her keys from her jacket pocket. "No classes for me tomorrow. How about you?"

"I have one class. See you sometime this week, though."

We waved and she got in her truck and I in my Jeep.

It rained all through the night, not the pounding rain I could hear on my roof but a gentle light steady rain. When I left for school the next morning the rain had stopped but it was foggy and overcast with the sky a uniform muddy gray.

My class was scheduled to end at two in the afternoon and Lily had a faculty meeting scheduled for one. After her meeting she was planning to come over for dinner, and I was cooking spaghetti with turkey meatballs. This was one of my few culinary attempts. I also had a bottle of red wine we were going to sample.

I stretched my arms and looked up at the clock on the

wall of my classroom. It was one thirty and I was done with my work.

"Are you finished too?"

I turned to the woman sitting on my left. At the beginning of the semester Debbie had been quiet and unwilling to offer anything in the nature of communication but after I picked her as my lab partner she gradually opened up and now seemed comfortable talking with me. She was thin and pale, with a grown-out perm that needed some attention, and I often thought that if she had a better haircut and a little makeup she would be attractive. She also needed some self-esteem.

The week before she had shyly told me she was not going to continue in the horticulture program but was going to the technical college in the fall for the culinary arts program. "Cooking is what I really love, but I can use my horticulture training because some restaurants are starting their own gardens for locally grown organic produce."

I started to ask Debbie about her plans for the summer when I was suddenly interrupted by screams, shouting and running footsteps.

Our instructor, who was bent over correcting lab reports, leaped to his feet, yanked open the door and stepped into the hall. Somebody shouted at him and he came back in and carefully closed the door behind him and stood there looking confused and upset.

"The Administration Building." He nervously pushed back his thinning brown hair. "Shots were fired."

The Administration Building was where Lily's meeting was being held. I jumped up. The instructor put out his hands. "We don't know what's going on out there—"

I bolted for the door.

"Julie, come back here!"

I ran out into the hall and down the stairs joining the crowd of students pouring out of their classrooms.

Someone behind me fell hard against me, and I reached for the handrail to catch my balance.

Outside, I stared across the campus to the Administration Building unable to believe what I was seeing. At least six squad cars were lined up in front of the building with their lights flashing, more were coming, and police were swarming everywhere while an ambulance pulled up, its siren wailing. A large crowd of onlookers had formed and the police had spread out trying to form a line to hold them back from approaching the building.

I stood on my tiptoes and strained to see over the crowd. "What happened?"

A man turned his head and spoke over his shoulder. "Some nut shot up the place."

The woman with him turned around to me. "I heard he burst into a meeting and opened fire."

"Is he still in there?"

The man shook his head. "I heard he shot himself when the police arrived."

I made my way around to the edge of the crowd and then pushed my way to the front. A group of faculty members were huddled together off to the side of the building protected by police. Among them I saw Vivian, the history professor I had met at the brew pub after the concert.

I waved and shouted to get her attention. "Vivian, where's Lily?"

"Step back please." A police officer motioned for me to step back.

"It's all right, I know her." I tried to step around him.

Vivian was shaking her head. "She's hurt, Julie. So are Professor Read and Professor Dunn."

"What happened to Lily?" I screamed.

The police officer moved in front of me.

Vivian bit her lip. "I don't know."

I pulled my keys from my jacket pocket and took off

running toward the student parking lot. I found my Jeep, jumped into it and sped out of the lot to the hospital where I knew they'd be taking her. The road outside the college was clogged with cars as police tried to divert them away from the college. As we crept along I became more and more agitated. What had happened to Lily?

We had finally found each other. Now she might be taken away from me. Hopelessly stuck in traffic I gripped the steering wheel as tears ran down my face, the screams of sirens piercing the air.

CHAPTER THIRTY-ONE

I rushed into the emergency room, disoriented and not knowing who to approach about Lily. A severe-looking older woman sat behind a counter to the left of me. She wore a pale blue lab jacket and a nametag that read "Violet."

"A woman was brought here after the shooting at Northbrook. Elisabeth de Gramont."

Violet peered at me over her bifocals. "How are you related? I assume you are family."

"She has no family here. I'm a close friend."

"Have a seat over there." She nodded toward a waiting area. I was dismissed.

I found an empty steel chair with a vinyl-covered seat, one of many in a long line arranged against the wall. Other occupants of the chairs ignored me as they listlessly paged through magazines or sat staring into space.

But across from me a crowd of people stood animatedly talking together and surrounding a man I remembered as David Hansen who had ended the orchestra rehearsal the night of the snowstorm. A woman in the group detached herself from them and rushed over to me. It was Jackie, the oboe player and partner of Vivian. I hadn't seen her since our meal together at the brew pub after our concert.

"Julie, Lily's okay. She's going to be okay."

I was filled with relief. She was alive. She was safe. "I'm not family, I don't think they'll let me see her or tell me anything about her condition."

"What you have to do is say you are a cousin or niece, something like that."

"It's too late for that. Is Vivian here? I saw her standing outside the Administration Building with other faculty members and thought she was all right."

"They brought them all here just to be checked out." Jackie sat down in an empty chair next to me and leaned over. "I can tell you what Vivian knows about Lily. By the way, you know it was Alan who was the shooter."

"I didn't know but I'm not surprised." After my terrified ride to the hospital I felt dizzy and my head was pounding. I was thinking only of Lily.

"He was a real crazy." She went on briskly, "Anyway, he fired a couple of shots over their heads, he had a handgun of some kind, then he aimed it at Professor Read. Lily was sitting in front of her and when he fired she grabbed Lily and pulled her to the floor."

Jackie unzipped her red fleece jacket and continued as I stared at her in horror. "Lily was unconscious when they took her out but Vivian thought she wasn't shot. Maybe hit her head. Professor Read was bleeding from the arm. I guess a bullet struck her, and Professor Dunn hurt his ankle trying to get away." She sighed. "Otherwise the rest weren't physically harmed. But what a terrible emotional experience!"

Perhaps the fact that Jackie, who was considered part of the group of relatives, was now talking intimately with me added to my stature because a nurse in scrubs with a stethoscope slung around her neck approached me.

"Are you here for Elisabeth de Gramont?"

I jumped up. "Yes, I am."

"She's been taken up to the third floor to be admitted. I can't say if you can see her. You'll have to talk to the staff there."

Jackie stood up and started to move away. "I think Vivian should be done now." She turned back. "I'm sure Lily will be okay."

After she walked away I hurried down the hall, looking around for the lobby and the elevators. A couple wearing matching Packers jackets was waiting for the elevator and stepped in ahead of me when it arrived. I waited impatiently for them to get off on the second floor.

On the third floor I approached the nurses' station where three nurses were huddled together in a discussion over a chart. One of them, a middle-aged woman looked up and then came over to me. I recited my prepared speech wondering if I should identify myself as Lily's cousin.

"I'm here to see Elisabeth de Gramont. They told me in the emergency room that she was admitted to this floor." I hesitated, "She has no family here, I'm her closest friend."

"Why don't you give me your name and then you can wait down at the end of the hall where there's a waiting area. We just got her and are getting her settled." She smiled and pointed down the hall.

Grateful for not being dismissed I obediently walked down to an area in front of tall windows overlooking the parking lot. Looking out I could see my Jeep in the distance. There were more vinyl-covered chairs in this room although these were heavier, more luxurious and designed to imitate leather lounge chairs. I sat down and put my head back. I must have closed my eyes because someone was standing in front of me talking. My eyes flew open. It was the kindly nurse who had spoken to me earlier. Her nametag read "Anita. RN."

"Julie Burke?"

"Yes." I stood up.

"We told Elisabeth you're here, and she wants to see you."

As we walked down the hall together she explained, "She has a concussion and a laceration on the back of her head. They put in four stitches. We're keeping her overnight but she can go home tomorrow. She may have a headache and sensitivity to noise and light for several days."

I remembered a teammate of mine on the basketball team suffering a concussion when a ball hit her in the head. She'd been out for over a week.

We stopped in front of a room and Nurse Anita entered first.

"Elisabeth, you have a visitor." She stepped aside and then discreetly withdrew leaving the door slightly ajar.

Lily turned her head toward me as I approached the bed. Her face was pale against her dark hair on the pillow.

"Julie, I asked for you. Why am I here?"

She extended her hand toward me and I pulled a chair over and then sat down taking her hand.

"Do you remember Alan coming into your meeting with a gun?"

"Yes, he pointed it at me and then I don't remember anything else."

"From what I was told Vickie pulled you down to save you both from being shot and you hit your head."

"Is Vickie all right?"

At this moment the door was pushed open and Vickie walked in. I stood up and stepped aside as she crossed the room to Lily's bed. Her jacket was draped over her shoulders and a large bandage covered her upper left arm.

"Hi Julie. Lily, they tell me you're going to be fine, just a bump on the head."

"Vickie, you saved my life."

"Oh, let's not exaggerate." Vickie waved her hand in a gesture of dismissal but nevertheless looked rather proud.

Lily looked up at Vickie's arm. "Did he hit you? Was anyone else hurt?"

"Just grazed my arm, a flesh wound. Professor Dunn twisted his ankle, only a sprain." She added with a grin, "He always was clumsy."

Lily frowned. "Whatever made Alan think he would ever be considered for your job?"

"I have no idea. I probably should have done something about him earlier. Well, it's all over now. You know he shot himself when the police arrived."

Her eyes widened. "No, I didn't. Are you sure your arm is going to be all right?"

"Oh yes." She gazed at Lily. "I better go so you can rest. By the way, classes are canceled tomorrow."

I spoke for the first time. "How are you getting home?"

"My graduate student, Allie, is waiting downstairs, she'll drive me."

Vickie leaned over, lightly kissed Lily's forehead, straightened up and started for the door. As she passed me she added. "Take care of her, Julie."

I sat in the chair next to Lily and took her hand in mine. "You can go home tomorrow. You'll stay with me for a few days until you feel better. We can stop at your place on the way and pick up whatever you need."

"I'd like that." Lily was having trouble keeping her eyes open.

"I'll be back tomorrow to take you home." Lily squeezed my hand as I leaned down and kissed her on the forehead where Vickie had kissed her.

As I walked down the hall from Lily's room the floor was quiet and no one was in the nurses' station. I rode down in the elevator alone, walked out the front entrance and stopped to look around me. Dusk had arrived and a light rain was falling.

As I unlocked the door of my Jeep I was overcome with feelings of fatigue and hunger and such a sense of unreality that I wondered if the events of this day had really happened.

CHAPTER THIRTY-TWO

"Julie, what are you doing on campus?"

I turned to see Vickie on the walk behind me. Her short burgandy-colored wool jacket and black slacks were similar to what she wore to our first orchestra rehearsal, which now seemed so long ago.

"School's over—so what are you doing here?" she asked.

"I came over to the bookstore to buy a text for one of my summer school classes." I held up the bookstore bag.

Vickie ignored the bag. "Are you interested in joining me for a farewell drink?"

"Yes, of course."

"How about Tosca? Meet me there." Vickie walked on.

Twenty minutes later I found her at the same table as the last time we were here. Maybe it was her special table, reserved for her. As I sat down she was slowly removing her jacket.

"How's your arm?" I could see she was having trouble with her left arm.

"Oh fine, almost healed. I'll have a scar, a reminder of what happened."

Tony appeared, his usual dapper self and smelling of his signature lotion, bearing a martini for Vickie and a glass of wine for me.

"I've given up on you as a martini drinker," Vickie said smiling, "I ordered wine for you."

I picked up the glass. "Thank you, it isn't that I don't like martinis, it's just that…"

Vickie raised her hand to stop me. "Never mind, I understand." She started to pick up her glass and then paused. "How is Lily doing?"

"Good. She doesn't have any more headaches and she had the stitches taken out a few days ago."

"We're having dinner together tomorrow night." She looked at me. "Did she tell you?"

"Yes, of course."

Vickie took a sip of her martini. "So, are you two lovers, partners for life, or what?"

I pushed my wineglass around on the napkin. "Both."

Vickie shook her head. "You and Lily are so sweet and easygoing everyone will take advantage of you."

She looked across the room, lost in thought. "I made a mistake with Lily, she's a wonderful person."

She looked back at me. "What's up for this summer?"

"Lily's teaching a summer school course, and I'm taking two classes and interning at the field station and then we're taking a vacation together." I paused. "She's moving in with me. Sharing my home."

Vickie nodded, emptied her glass and signaled to Tony. "Did you know Professor Fox is retiring after this next year?"

"Professor Fox? Is he in your department?"

Vickie looked exasperated. "No, he's head of the English department."

"Oh, I remember, the one who broke his leg."

"That's right. Don't you understand what that means?"

Tony set down a martini and another wine for me. Vickie waited until he left.

"Lily is in line to replace him. She'll be in an important position at the college." Vickie shook her head. "She probably doesn't quite get it, but she has a lot of support. Everyone feels she deserves the position, and I'm certain she will be selected."

Finally it sunk in. I was so happy and proud for Lily that I just sat there and beamed.

She leaned back and examined her watch. "I have so much to do what with packing and deciding what not to take with me."

I finished my first glass of wine, set it aside and picked up the new one. I asked, "Are you taking your piano?"

"No, too expensive to move it halfway across the country and besides I'm not sure where I'll be living." She lifted her martini. "My friend has been looking at homes for us." She caught herself. "For me, and she's narrowed it down to three. I'm flying out there next week to look them over."

So Vickie possibly had someone new in her life. My mind was on the piano.

"Did you sell your piano?"

Vickie sighed. "Not yet, I want to advertise it but haven't had the time. Why do you ask? Know someone who might be interested?"

"Yes, I am."

"I didn't know you played. I'll give you a good deal, it would be a relief to sell it now and besides, it'll look good in your home."

She named a price which was not only reasonable, but a steal.

"I'll give you a check right now." I reached into my purse and took out a pen and blank check. I wrote it out and handed it to Vickie, who folded it and stuffed it in her purse without looking at it.

Vickie finished her martini, and picked up her purse. "I don't like long goodbyes. I'm going over and settle up with Tony. You stay here and finish your wine. And don't leave him any money, I'll take care of the tip."

Vickie stood up, put her hand on my shoulder, bent down and kissed my temple. "Take care of Lily."

I murmured. "Best of everything, Vickie."

I watched as she laid some bills on the bar for Tony, turned and walked out the door without looking back.

As I drove home I thought about Vickie and wondered what would have happened between us if I had not met Lily. Very likely nothing, Vickie was just not for me.

CHAPTER THIRTY-THREE

"Julia, this is your neighbor Dorothy."

I anxiously gripped the phone wondering if she was in trouble. She continued, "I'm going on a trip for two weeks and now it turns out that the couple I thought would be able to watch my house is going to Nebraska to visit their daughter and her family. Anyway, I was wondering if you would be here, only to check on the house. My yard service will take care of anything, well, no snow now I guess, but if a big branch fell down or something like that. I don't worry about flooding. I never had water in my basement." She added, "Neither did your aunt."

I was relieved to hear that. She named the dates she would be gone. "Yes, of course I can. I'll be here taking some classes in summer school."

"Good, I'll bring my house key over."

"I can come over and get it. Is this a good time?"

"Why thank you."

I walked around to Dorothy's back door. The door immediately swung open.

"Come in."

Dorothy was wearing black slacks and a soft green cotton turtleneck. "I'm glad I got you, I have an early dinner planned with friends."

I stood inside the kitchen door.

"Sit down." Dorothy motioned toward her round oak kitchen table. "I haven't been on a trip for several years. Pepe didn't like the kennel and the woman who took care of him unfortunately died four years ago. I won't be getting a new dog until I get back."

I had a brief vision of Lily and me tending a Chihuahua when Dorothy had the yen to travel again.

"May I ask where you're going?"

"Ireland. George never wanted to go there. I am so excited. This is a travel group I've been with before. All my age, mostly single or widowed." She added, "And a few couples. I'm going to check on my Irish family names. I might even find some long-lost relatives."

She cocked her head and looked at me. "You're Irish aren't you? I know your father was. What about your mother?"

"She too." I had a vague memory of my aunt not approving of my mother's kind of Irish.

Dorothy handed me her back door key on a keychain from the Green River Botanical Gardens.

"I saw the article about your aunt's new education center at the Nature Center. Admirable of her, the donation."

I remembered Dorothy telling me she was a Friend of the Green River Botanical Gardens. I suspected that the Nature Center was a little too rustic for her.

When I returned home I was hanging Dorothy's key on my key rack when my phone rang.

"Julie, this is Beth. I'm just leaving town and wondered if we could get together. I have some news about Amy. Do you have any classes?"

"No Beth, the semester is over."

"How is the coffee place on Ohio Street, Great Grounds? Do you know it?"

"Yes, I can come right over."

On the way to the coffee shop I tried to figure out what the news about Amy could be. From Beth's somber tone it didn't sound good. The worst news would be that they found her body somewhere.

When I arrived, Beth's Ford was parked in front and she waved to me from a table inside. I got a mug of the mild coffee of the day and joined her at a small table next to the window.

Beth looked tired, she had grooves in her face I hadn't seen before and there were dark circles under her eyes. She moved her purse out of the way on the table.

"Do you remember Nicole from the New Year's Eve party?"

"Yes, I do. I heard she moved to Florida."

"We weren't close but I had a brief note from her. She and a friend were in Key West and there was Amy tending bar in some women's place. She thought I should know."

So she did take off for a warmer climate. "Have you told your mother?"

"Yes." Beth sighed. "She's alternating between relief that Amy is safe and anger that she never contacted us."

I tried to think of something that might explain Amy's behavior but it seemed typical of Amy's selfishness and disregard for other people's feelings. I was sorry for the women in Key West with Amy running around loose down there.

"I came up here to talk with the detective. Of course, the case is closed. He was very nice about it all." Beth stood up. "I'm going to get a refill. Want one?"

"No thanks." Even the mild coffee of the day was too strong for me.

When Beth sat down and picked up her coffee mug I saw that her hand was shaking.

"Between Amy's disappearance and the situation at the lab I am emotionally drained."

I waited in silence and then asked. "How is everything with the lab?"

"Terrible. They lost several accounts and don't seem to be acquiring any new ones." Beth took a sip of her coffee. "I'm looking for something else. We think they might lose the lawsuit, even if it will take a while."

"Yes, Ginger and Cindy are thinking of moving." I didn't mention Florida.

Beth flipped her hair back. "I wouldn't know because they don't confide in me." She looked out the window. "I suppose the cost of living is cheap up here."

Oh no, I thought, don't let her move here. As I tried to formulate an answer Beth continued.

"I couldn't live here. Two weeks and I would be crazy." She pulled up her jacket sleeve and looked at her watch. "I better get going. I know the days are getting longer now but I want to be back before dark." She looked at me critically. "I guess for you moving up here was the right decision."

Out on the sidewalk we had an awkward farewell.

"Thanks for your help, Julie." Beth started toward her car.

"I'm sorry Beth. I wish I could have done more."

She waved, got in her car and pulled away.

As I drove home I thought about all the people Amy

had hurt. Mary, Vickie, Lily, her own mother and sister, and who knew how many others. How lucky I was to find Lily. She was coming over to be with me for the weekend and I couldn't wait.

CHAPTER THIRTY-FOUR

I awoke to the chirping of birds. Before going to bed I had opened my bedroom window following a lovely day of temperatures in the upper sixties. The cool evening air was refreshing after a winter of closed windows. But the birds continued their competitive songs and somewhere in the distance a barking dog made sleep difficult. I rolled over and looked at my bedside clock. It was almost five.

I pulled the covers over my head hoping to fall asleep but finally gave up and went downstairs. As I sat waiting for my coffeemaker to finish I looked around the kitchen at the linoleum floor, harvest yellow appliances and yellow wall phone. When Lily moved in I wanted her to feel she was truly sharing the house, not just a guest here. This kitchen badly needed some updates. I would let Lily choose what should be done. She had good taste, and it would be an opportunity for her to become involved in decisions about the house.

I carried my coffee into my new office intending to pay some bills. When I opened my desk drawer I saw the piece of paper I had taken on my clipboard to Vickie's house the day I visited her garden with the measurements of the fishpond, and beneath them my scrawled grocery shopping list. I sat there holding the paper in my hand. The day I went to see her garden now seemed so long ago. Vickie had put her house up for sale and had left town leaving her garden behind. I dropped the paper in the wastebasket.

Last night Lily had attended a retirement party for one of her colleagues. I remembered Vickie telling me that Professor Fox was retiring next year and now realized what an important position replacing Professor Fox would be for Lily. I was determined to get my master's degree, not only because I was so interested in my studies but now I also wanted Lily to be proud of me. Perhaps there might be a doctorate in my future.

After my breakfast I got in my Jeep and drove out to the edge of town. The sun emerged from behind a cloud as I entered Calvary Cemetery. The freshly mowed grass was looking lushly green and people had started placing flowers and other offerings on the graves. Before Memorial Day I intended to get something for my aunt. I decided an artificial arrangement would be best; it wouldn't need watering, especially in the hot summer months when real flowers would die. Red roses would be best; she wasn't a person who liked pink flowers. I stood before the red granite stone she had picked out several years before she died. My aunt intended to have what she wanted, not what someone else chose for her.

I knelt down to brush some fallen leaves from the base of her marker. Looking around, I saw that I was alone in the cemetery. My religious education had been haphazard so I wasn't sure if those who were supposedly up in heaven knew what was happening down here, but I addressed my aunt. "Aunt Margaret, Laura didn't leave you, there was an accident. I know you both would've spent the rest of your lives together. I'm sorry it didn't happen that way. I've found someone that I love very much and intend to stay with her the rest of my life."

I stopped and stood up. This was enough. My aunt was never too sentimental.

I wondered about the grave of Laura Gorman, but of course June and her niece would be tending it.

My aunt's father and mother, and grandparents I didn't remember, were also buried here. I looked across at their faded marble markers. My father was not buried here. As a child I remembered that that had been another occasion of family dissent when my mother insisted on having him buried in her family cemetery in her hometown.

It had been over a year now since my aunt's funeral. Afterward the women in her church had put on a lunch in the church basement. Never having attended her church with my aunt and not knowing her friends, I had stood around awkwardly, sensing they were pointing me out as Margaret's only relative, a niece from out of town. As soon as I could, I escaped, but before I headed back to Milwaukee I drove over to my aunt's house and parked in front for a last look at it. I was sure it was going to be left to her church, and I didn't expect to ever return to Green River or see my aunt's home again. How wrong I was.

Back home in the kitchen I looked up at the yellow electric wall clock and made a mental note to replace it. Nine o'clock, maybe not too early to call Lily.

As soon as her phone rang she picked up. "Julie, this is so amazing. I was just about to call you but wasn't sure if it was too early."

"Definitely not. How was the party?"

"Wonderful, Emily loved it, she's so happy to be retiring. They're moving to Florida."

"Would you want to retire?"

Lily laughed. "Oh, certainly not. I love my work. I'd like to see you. Maybe we could go for a bike ride."

"I'm going right out and put the bike rack on my Jeep. Let's try the trail that winds through the park. See you soon."

"Bye, darling."

No one had ever called me darling. Not my aunt and certainly not my mother.

***

Later that day Lily was reclining on the soon-to-be-banished floral couch. She had just taken a shower and was wrapped in her heavy white terry cloth robe while she examined the brochure with the itinerary for our trip. Across the room Vickie's piano stood in the corner near the bay windows.

I sat on the floor next to the couch going through last year's bills and receipts, which I had saved for a year and was now discarding. These were from April of last year. As I looked through them it was hard to believe what my life had been like thirteen months earlier. There were receipts for my apartment rental, electricity, gas and a new fleece jacket for spring. Recently I had begun wearing the fleece jacket and had put away my ski jacket and parka. Here was a receipt for cleaning the valves on my horn.

"I guess it's time to get my horn cleaned."

Lily stretched. "You're right, this couch isn't very comfortable." She looked up from the brochure. "Time for a COA on my flute. While we are on our trip will be a good time."

"What's a COA?"

"Cleaning, oiling and adjustment. Maybe you could also take your horn. I have it done in Green Bay. They're very capable."

"Sounds good."

"It's too bad there aren't any duets for horn and flute." Lily looked back down at the brochure.

"I'm not aware of any, and I don't want to get a woodwind quintet together. Too many diverse personalities."

"So true." She raised her head. "I have an idea. Why don't we buy a pair of recorders? Two altos or an alto and a soprano. There's a tremendous amount of literature for them."

"Great idea. I'd love to learn a new instrument."

Lily waved the brochure. "Julie, I know this is early to make our plans since we haven't gone on this trip, but I thought of a place we might visit next year."

"Where is that?"

"I thought perhaps Ireland. You haven't been there, have you?"

"No, but I would love to go there." I laughed. "Be

prepared, you know our neighbor Dorothy will be full of advice for us. She really liked Ireland."

I pushed the bills aside. "I sent June Gorman the newsletter from the Nature Center with the article about the butterfly house. She has a niece with two children and they're excited about coming to see it this summer."

"That's wonderful." Lily paused. "How sad Laura's disappearance was for your aunt, but finding her was closure for June and her family."

Amy Leland's disappearance had been solved but I felt Lily should know what happened to her. "Beth, Amy's older sister, was up here and we met for coffee. The case is closed because someone wrote Beth that she spotted Amy tending bar in Key West."

Lily shook her head. "Shame on her. And to think she never let her family know she was all right."

There was silence and when I looked up Lily dropped the brochure on the floor and patted the couch next to her. "Come over here."

I stood up, sat down on the edge of the couch and put my hand on Lily's temple.

"Your hair is still damp from your shower."

Lily raised her arms and put them around my neck. Her robe fell open as she pulled me down and kissed me.

I could only murmur "Lily, dear Lily" as I slipped my hand inside her robe. She closed her eyes and lay back on the pillow.

Thirteen months ago I had been hurt, lonely and with no plans for my future. Now, everything in my life had changed.

TWO MONTHS LATER...

I could feel the plane begin its descent. I watched out the window as we approached Amsterdam's Schipol Airport.

"Look." I pointed out the window. Below us the Amstel River, the canals and the buildings of Amsterdam were coming closer. As Lily put her hand on my knee and leaned over to peer out the window I was still thrilled by the touch of her hand and her closeness.

"You know I think we should buy our recorders here.

The Dutch make a fine Coolsma recorder. I believe they're made in Utrecht."

I smiled and nodded. "Good idea, I'd like that."

"Vivian gave me a list of places to see." It seemed Vivian and Jackie had been here two years ago, and when we were at their cottage the week before, Vivian and Lily had discussed the trip and their experiences here while Jackie and I were out canoeing.

Lily leaned closer. "She also gave me the names of some women's clubs they visited." She sat back. "And Vivian said they want to have us up to their cottage again when we get back. The weather should still be warm."

"Lily, would you like for us to own a cottage? It would be on a lake for the summer but also with a place to snowshoe or cross-country ski in the winter. I am picturing a fireplace blazing away."

"And us playing our recorders in front of it."

"Yes, among other things. We could look around when we get back."

I silently thanked my aunt for the gift of her house which led to my moving to Green River, embarking on a new career, joining the orchestra and meeting Lily.

I turned toward Lily and she reached over and took my hand. As we leaned back in our seats preparing for the landing we looked at each other. Our life together had begun.

Bella Books, Inc.

Women. Books. Even Better Together.

P.O. Box 10543
Tallahassee, FL 32302

Phone: 800-729-4992
www.bellabooks.com